THE BITTER PATH OF DEATH

By the same author
Gone To Her Death

The Bitter Path of Death

PIERRE AUDEMARS

WALKER AND COMPANY

NEW YORK

First published in the United States of America in 1982 by
the Walker Publishing Company, Inc.

ISBN: 0-8027-5484-8

Library of Congress Catalog Card Number: 82-60217

Printed in the United States of America

10   9   8   7   6   5   4   3   2   1

To
my wife
and my sons —
with love,
gratitude,
admiration
and
respect.

The depth and dream of my desire,
   The bitter paths wherein I stray —
Thou knowest Who hast made the Fire,
   Thou knowest Who hast made the Clay.

My New-cut Ashlar
Rudyard Kipling

PROLOGUE

In the days when all the years of devoted toil and labour given so generously by his chronicler had finally brought M. Pinaud to the peak of his eminence, they were in the habit of meeting frequently for periods of intelligent conversation.

It is an indisputable fact that these interesting discussions were generally inspired, prolonged and even enriched by the contents of some of the bottles of excellent wines and liqueurs whose purchase became a simple matter with the frequent arrival of so many large royalty cheques. But to their eternal credit these two gentlemen always made valiant and praiseworthy efforts together to decide which noteworthy or remarkable case merited the honour of being chosen for the next publication.

On this particular occasion his chronicler sipped slowly and delicately, and with all the reverence it fully deserved, at a claret which had been bottled some twenty years previously.

'What about the Swiss master-watchmaker and that dead jeweller in the Rue de La Paix?' he asked thoughtfully.

M. Pinaud had already emptied his glass.

'But that was years ago —' he objected.

'Does that matter?'

'I was young and ignorant –'

'This wine too – *mirabile dictu* – was also once young. And years ago we were both ignorant. That is not only the advantage but also the privilege of age. One learns.'

'But that was no case. I did nothing. That was one of my failures.'

Instead of answering, his chronicler sipped and savoured the incredible contents of his glass with due solemnity until it was empty. M. Pinaud reached for the bottle and refilled both glasses.

'Thank you,' said his chronicler politely. 'You said failure. There is no such word, provided a man tries honestly and fairly, and gives the best of himself to what he is trying to do. You remember what the English poet said. If you can meet with triumph and disaster, and treat these two impostors just the same.'

Over the years, it will be observed by the intelligent and discerning reader, he had tended to grow somewhat didactic. He also gave Mr. Pinaud no time to reply, but continued to declaim with an eloquence which – under the circumstances – was hardly surprising.

'Whatever you say, that case had interest and human appeal. What else do people want when they read? And why do they read?'

No-one answered his questions, so he answered them himself.

'To escape from the monotony of their daily lives – to be interested, excited and entertained – to lose themselves, for a few blessed hours, in a world of make-believe.'

M. Pinaud listened entranced. He had consumed, as usual, rather more than his share of that remarkable claret, and therefore it is hardly surprising to relate that all the qualities conducive to good and sympathetic listening – patience, tolerance and understanding – all seemed to be merging and swarming and surging chaotically within him, as if floating in ecstasy on a sea of alcohol . . .

Besides, this was the expert talking. Whatever his faults – and he had many – no-one had ever denied that his chronicler not only knew how to write but also could relate a convincing and compelling tale.

'All literature is an escape, particularly crime fiction. It is so much easier in this life to read about something rather than make the effort to do it.

'And most people – in spite of what one reads in the newspapers to-day – are basically good and honest. The majority like to believe that justice eventually triumphs over evil – or else what is the point of religion – that the criminal is finally caught and the murderer punished.

'In their monotonous daily lives, normal and average citizens rarely encounter either of these types. In a book they can all share the excitement and the entertainment without making the slightest effort.'

It could be, M. Pinaud reflected gravely, that all the qualities conducive to good and convincing eloquence were also merging and swarming and surging and floating on another sea of alcohol in a different mind and stomach – there were enough empty bottles on the sideboard – as his chronicler continued to hold forth interminably on his favourite topic.

But then – characteristically – he dismissed this thought as unworthy and continued to listen with grave attention and befitting gratitude. After all, this one had worked for a lifetime to make him famous.

They talked and listened, drank and smoked too much, and thoroughly enjoyed themselves. And the subject of the next book was decided and approved.

Once he had gone, M. Pinaud poured himself a final glass of wine and went to sit by his blazing log-fire.

Each one of the hundred he had laid and lit was always different, the pictures he could see in the flames and red-hot embers never the same.

He drank his wine slowly and sat there, dreaming and remembering the days when he had been young.

He heard once again the words of comfort he had spoken to the pregnant Capet daughter, he shivered at the memory of how Madame Laroche's threats had terrified him and he bowed his head in humility and thankfulness that he had been given the strength and the courage to go on, to try again and again . . .

ONE

The man was seated on a low stool at one end of the dining-room table, a standard-lamp with a powerful bulb at his elbow. In front of him, on the edges of a square of thick white paper, were two shallow china dishes containing watchmaker's fine tools.

He was dark, with a broad and high forehead and a long and dominant nose. He reached out to pick up a small jewelled box from the table. His hands were incredibly beautiful, with long tapering nails, the second and third fingers of the same length.

The box was rectangular, only centimetres high, made of gold and encrusted with diamonds and pearls. He held it delicately in one hand and with the other thumb moved a jewelled slide at one end.

There was a whirr and a click, as a small oval and enamelled lid on the top snapped open on a hinge. A tiny bird sprang upright and began to pivot around and sing, so realistically one could almost imagine that its miniature beak opened and closed in time with the liquid bird-notes which emanated from the bellows set below the open-work gold grill, tooled with lace-like fragility, above which it turned.

The bird's eyes were diamonds, its beak gold. Its features were artistically painted and lacquered, blue, green and gold.

The boy was kneeling on the carpet at the side of the table, watching and listening and obviously completely fascinated. He was in his teens, already broad and powerfully built and showing the promise of great strength. There could be no mistaking as to who he was: here were the same features and the same hands.

The bird sang. The boy watched, his very soul in his eyes. The man pulled down a watchmaker's magnifying-glass from a wire across his forehead to his eye, held the box closer and examined the moving bird very carefully.

The young girl sat in a comfortable armchair in front of a small electric fire, busily knitting a baby's vest.

She did not even look up when the song started, but stirred restlessly, obviously pregnant. Her slender and powerful hands did not falter in their delicate and practised dexterity.

Here again the family likeness was unmistakable, although the delicacy of her features, coupled with a mass of rich auburn hair, gave her an astonishing beauty.

The song ended. The bird folded down on hinged feet into its recess in the grill, and the lid snapped shut.

The man pushed his glass up on to his forehead and looked across the room at his daughter. A spasm of pain constricted his features but he did not say anything.

The boy moved his position.

'Every time I see and hear one I wonder if I am dreaming. It does not seem possible – it is like a miracle.'

Both love and tenderness vibrated in the man's voice

as he replied.

'It is a miracle, Jean — a miracle of craftsmanship. There is only one family in the world who can make them. A father and seven sons — a unique combination of skill and talent. Only one can paint, lacquer and cement those tiny feathers on the birds. Only one has mastered the art of treating skin to make the miniature bellows supple enough to work.

'The mechanism is fine watchmaker's work, as complicated in some ways as a minute repeater, a *grande sonnerie* or clock-watch, which strikes the hours in passing, a split-second chronograph or a perpetual calendar which changes automatically to February 29th every fourth year. These are the kind of watches I frequently have to clean and repair.'

He put the box back on the table very carefully and picked up a second one. This was made of platinum, with a magnificent opal set into the lid.

'The mechanism in one of these boxes,' he continued, 'consists of about three hundred parts. There is a wheel-train driven by the mainspring, one of them, the pin-wheel, activating the levers which pump air into the bellows for the song. And there are some very delicate cams engaging with articulated levers. Each bird has three levers inside its body — one to open and close the beak, one to raise and lower the wings and one to turn it as it sings. That one I cleaned and oiled last night. It seems to be all right now.'

He inserted a key through an aperture in the base and wound the mainspring on the second box. Then he moved the slide. The lid sprang open, the bird pivoted upright and the song began.

After a few seconds there was an audible click. The song ended suddenly, the bird stopped moving

13

and remained upright.

The man reached for a screwdriver and pulled the glass down to his eye.

'It may have been dropped,' he said as he began to dismantle the box. 'In that case it could be a tooth bent on a pinion or a pivot jammed in a cracked jewel. Or it may just be wear on one of the cams. I can write to Switzerland for a new one to-morrow.'

As he talked his hands and fingers continued to move with incredible speed and skill.

The boy shifted his position again, but not his eyes.

'Father, how soon can I leave school here and go to learn watchmaking at Le Sentier?'

The four base screws were placed on the white paper and the plate removed. With tweezers the whole mechanism was delicately eased out of the box. The screwdriver was exchanged for a far smaller one, the forefinger steadying the circular top, the thumb and second finger turning the milled shaft as the microscopic screw began to turn.

The man's hands did not cease to work as he spoke.

'Are you sure, Jean — quite sure — that this is what you want to do?'

'Positive.'

'Seven years is a long time. Especially when one is young. For the first two they only let you file and make tools. You may get discouraged and lose sight of your objective.'

'Not me.'

The man laid the mechanism down delicately on its side on the paper and pushed the glass up on to his forehead. He held his head with the lift of an eagle and now there was pride as well as love and tenderness in his voice.

'No — you would never do that. You are my son.'

It was evening. The rush-hour in the city was over. Very little noise disturbed the quietness of that room in their second-floor flat.

For a moment the silence seemed to surge in a wave of love and understanding, a moment unforgettable in the intensity of its feeling . . .

Then the man lowered his glass, picked up his screwdriver and the mechanism, and continued to work.

'I would advise you to wait a little longer,' he said. 'Everyone agrees that the future of the mechanical watch is doubtful. There has been an amazing development in electronics in the past few years. I have been told that the watch of the future will be powered by a miniature battery and no longer by a mainspring, and instead of hands illuminated figures will indicate the time. To master this technology will obviously need an entirely different training.'

'That will take a long time.'

'Perhaps not so long as you think, Jean. As you know, after the war I had to leave the *Vallée de Joux* with two young children. There was no work for me there, even with my training and my skill, because of the crisis in the watch trade.

'I came here to Paris and I was fortunate in finding employment. I was prepared to clean and repair fine-quality watches for eight hours a day and also to work here at home until midnight and during week-ends at this kind of extra work so that you and your sister could have a better life and more opportunity than I ever had.'

He paused and sighed. The mechanism was now

15

partially dismantled, the bird lying, disconnected and strangely pathetic, on its side on the white paper, next to wheels, cams, screws and levers.

'The future is really terribly uncertain, Jean.'

'That is what they say at school. But this is what I want to do. The masters are all drips — all except the woodwork man. He makes the other chaps watch me when I use a chisel or a plane. But I want to work in metal, not in wood.'

The man gestured towards the bird-box on the table in front of him.

'But how do you know that these will still be made in seven years?' he asked. 'Or even the type of watch you want to make or repair?'

'I don't. But this is what I want to do.'

Then Jean hesitated, as if finding it difficult to choose the right words.

'But this woodwork master — he is really the only one with any sense — he maintains that a skilled craftsman need never worry about earning his living, provided he works well and conscientiously and charges a fair and honest price.'

The man reached out with his tweezers and picked up a tiny lever from the white paper. He smiled as he lifted it to his eye, and his features softened and seemed to change completely.

'He sounds like a good type, this master of yours. I ought to meet him. We will discuss this matter properly over the week-end, Jean, when I am not so busy.'

The door opened and a lady came into the room.

She was middle-aged, but her figure was still slender and graceful. Her eyes were wise, tolerant and sad, pouched and lined with care. In the planes and contours of her features the astonishing beauty she had bequeathed to her daughter was still clearly apparent.

Her first glance was to the girl in the chair, but her words were addressed to her husband at the table.

'I am sorry to trouble you when you are so busy, dear, but do you think you could find a few moments to sharpen my kitchen knife for me?'

The man went on turning the lever slowly in front of his glass.

'Of course. But do you mean now?'

'Well, I wanted to cut the beef for dinner. It is the short thin one, but I find it blunt and the tip is bent. Someone must have been using it for nonsense.'

Jean spoke softly to his mother, without ever moving his eyes from the tiny lever.

'Why not borrow mine? Father is busy.'

'Yours, Jean? I did not know –'

'Yes – mine. I swopped a genuine Mafia knife from a chap at school. He went on holiday to Sicily and brought it back with him. Short and thin – just like yours.'

'Very well. Thank you.'

'I'll get it for you. I want to watch father.'

He stood upright from his kneeling position in one swift and fluid motion.

She looked at them both, with love, respect and toleration illuminating and transforming the tired and weary eyes.

The girl spoke for the first time as her brother left the room.

'Take care of that knife, mother – once it has been done – not to cut yourself. When I borrowed it last it was as sharp as a razor.'

17

'Thank you, Yvonne. I will be careful. Do not worry. I have been using sharp knives ever since I was married.'

Jean opened the door and handed the knife in its sheath to his mother.

Suddenly, unexpectedly and stridently, the front door-bell rang. They all jumped at the unexpected sound.

The man laid down his tweezers on the white paper, pushed the glass up on to his forehead and sighed in resignation. Then he straightened and sat upright on his stool.

'There is a screw somewhere on the carpet, Jean,' he said.

'Shall I look for it?' the boy asked eagerly. 'I found the last one —'

'No — no. It would not be courteous to our visitor. See who it is, please — and do not make him wait.'

The boy crossed to the window, lifted the curtain and looked down.

'There is a fine car outside,' he said, as if the information was important. No-one answered. Then he went out to open the front door.

The three people in the room waited in silence. A tension, almost palpable in its intensity, seemed to rise and spread and forbid them to speak.

The man still sat upright on his stool, his stare intent on his daughter. His wife stood rigidly still, holding the knife in its sheath in both clasped hands, her eyes closed. The girl Yvonne went on with her knitting.

Jean came back into the room almost immediately, his eyes bright with excitement.

'There is a chap outside who says his name is

18

Pinaud. He would like to speak to you on a matter of great importance.'

TWO

It all really began on that fine morning in early spring when M. Pinaud was summoned by M. le Chef to his beautiful office on the second floor of the grey building on the Quai d'Orsay.

He stood to attention, waiting respectfully, since in that gracious room there was only one chair.

M. le Chef looked up from its capacious depths, in which he had been seated, assiduously studying a single sheet of blank notepaper. This harmless idiosyncrasy, he was wont to maintain, enabled him to concentrate his thoughts in an orderly fashion.

M. Pinaud's opinion, which he naturally kept to himself, was that for such an intellect to demean itself in this way was both childish and unnecessary.

The shrewd eyes studied the tall and powerful figure standing in front of him. This young Pinaud had already solved enough remarkable cases to merit all his confidence. And also to be handed any and each of those which had all the indications of being completely insoluble.

By these methods the reputation of his department was far less likely to suffer. Moreover, any credit, fame or glory accruing from these astonishing and outstanding exploits came automatically, as is the way of the world, to him and his credit.

'Ah yes, Pinaud. Are you on anything special now?'

'Not at the moment, m'sieu.'

'Good. You have no doubt heard of Laroche, the celebrated jeweller in the Rue de la Paix?'

'Naturally, m'sieu.'

'Edmond Laroche, the owner, was found dead in his first-floor office last night. He had been stabbed in the back of his neck, at the base of his skull, with what was almost certainly a short thin knife. Death would have been instantaneous. The knife was withdrawn, so we have no weapon.

'We have no motive either. In fact, we have very little.'

He paused for a moment, and a fleeting smile touched the mobile mouth.

'But I am sure that this will not deter you in any way, Pinaud. To continue. Laroche was in the habit of closing his shop at the normal time in the evening when he set the alarm. Then he would go up to his office, which had a separate staircase beside the shop, leading up from an adjoining front door.

'There he would stay later, in order to interview special clients or trade repairers, salesmen and dealers – anyone and all the people who needed more time than he could give when he was busy in his shop.

Above the office is a small self-contained flat, which was used when his secretary or his manager had to work late.

'When he left at night to go back to his hotel-suite and finally double-locked this door an automatic signal at the nearest police-station recorded that the alarm was correctly set and in order. The stock in his safes must be worth millions.

21

'It was his custom to offer his visitors a drink. He was a drinking man himself. There was a liqueur-cabinet behind his desk.

'Last night the automatic signal did not function. The Inspector telephoned, but there was no answer. He sent a man to investigate. The side door was closed on its latch, but not double-locked.

'He forced it open and went upstairs. In the office he found the door of the cabinet open and the dead body of Laroche on the floor in front of it.'

M. le Chef paused and looked at M. Pinaud, waiting expectantly.

'Is that all, m'sieu?'

Again the fleeting smile came and went.

'There is not a great deal, is there?' But you have done wonders with less. I have every confidence in you, Pinaud.'

'Thank you, m'sieu.'

'One or two things might help. You had better go round to the morgue and have a look at him yourself. See what you think of the wound.

'And I would suggest that you go to the Rue de La Paix to interview a certain Louise de Granson, confidential secretary to the late Laroche, who works in her own private office adjoining his.

She may be able to give you some information, as she often used to stay late to help him.'

He leaned forward in his chair, pulled open a drawer in his desk and took out a sheet of paper.

'Here are a few notes about her – all we have been able to find out in the time. She seems reliable, had a very good education, and applied for the position five years ago with some remarkable references.

'According to her statement, two men came up last

22

night to Laroche's office after the shop was closed. She head their steps up the stairs and their voices when they spoke to him. She always left the door of her adjoining office ajar.

'Then, after they had gone, Laroche himself came into her office and told her not to wait but to go home. He was expecting another caller but said that he could manage on his own.

'One conclusion seems obvious to me, Pinaud — he would not have asked anyone he did not know or trust to go up to his office, nor turn his back on them to pour a drink. Small points like these might be of help to you, Pinaud.'

'You are quite right, m'sieu. They certainly will be. Thank you for your help.'

'It is my privilege. Good luck, Pinaud — and take care of yourself. Having killed once, a murderer has obviously very few scruples left.'

'I know. I have had experience of that. Do not worry, m'sieu. I will do my best.'

The doctor in the morgue was young, keen and obviously capable. His white overall was also spotlessly clean, which, considering the number of mutilated and bleeding corpses brought into his premises every day as a result of car accidents, was a fact that raised him high in M. Pinaud's esteem.

But in spite of his capabilities and his qualifications, he was unable to improve very much on M. le Chef's shrewd appraisal of the circumstances.

He led M. Pinaud into the vast refrigerated room with its rows of metal containers, stopped in front of one, opened it and drew back a sheet from the mortal remains of Edmond Laroche.

'I left his eyes open,' he said apologetically. 'He seemed to be staring so aggressively, even when he was dead, that I thought the implication of his character might be of interest to you in your investigation.'

'That was a very intelligent thought,' M. Pinaud commended him warmly. 'And very useful to me in that it confirms what I had already surmised. After all, a jeweller with his reputation, who could buy and assemble together a stock of magnificent and artistically mounted precious stones which brought people to admire from the ends of the earth, was bound to have been touched with arrogance. You have only to look at him now to confirm what I have said. Arrogant in life — arrogant even in death.

'Whether this has anything to do with his murder is for me to find out.'

He took one long, last and thoughtful look at the features beneath him, noting and committing to memory the high-bridged and dominant nose, the broad and intelligent forehead and the full and fleshy lips in a wide and sensual mouth.

'Only one blow was struck,' the doctor told him. 'A quick stab in the back of the neck, at the base of his skull. Death was instantaneous, and the knife withdrawn.'

'It was a knife?'

'Almost certainly. With a short thin blade.'

'Therefore the person with him — the murderer — must have been someone he knew, trusted and did not suspect. Or else he would never have turned his back to open the cabinet.'

'Agreed. He must have fallen forward as he died. He was lying face downward on the carpet in front of the cabinet when I arrived. The door was open.'

'What time was this?'

'I was summoned by the police at seven-thirty. By the time I had got there and finished my examination — about eight o'clock, I should think.'

'I see,' said M. Pinaud thoughtfully.

'Does that make any difference?'

'No. Not really. The important time is earlier — when these friends and acquaintances called to see him. And when he was lying dead on the floor and unable to double-lock the side door to activate the automatic alarm-signal. And when his murderer left the premises, quietly and unobtrusively, in exactly the same way that he or she had entered. Laroche could have been caught as he fell and lowered gently to the carpet. There would have been no noise.'

The young doctor looked at him with the awed respect that the exposition of such masterly principles of logical deduction fully deserved.

Already this one was famous. Soon he would become a legend.

'Of course,' he agreed enthusiastically, 'Then all you have to do is to interview and question —'

M. Pinaud eyed him with pity and compassion as he interrupted, castigating himself with characteristic severity even as he did so. Enthusiasm in the young was always a commendable virtue, and one well worthy of encouragement. But this one was very young and he did not understand.

'Considering that Laroche here only saw them there by appointment,' he said gently, 'and came down the stairs himself to draw the latch on the door when the bell rang — it will not be easy. I am afraid I cannot agree with your choice of words.'

The doctor looked suitably abashed. M. Pinaud

felt even more remorseful.

'Never mind,' he said cheerfully, and the quick and sudden smile transfigured the hard strong lines of his features. 'You are quite right. The impossible always takes a little longer – so the sooner I get on with it the better.

'Good-bye, doctor, and thank you for your help.'

On the ground floor, inside the famous shop, M. Pinaud looked around with approval at the crystal chandeliers, the velvet-embossed wallpaper and the mahogany show-cases, and felt his heavy boots sink into the luxurious pile carpet as he presented his credentials to M. Dubois, the manager.

'Ah yes,' murmured a muted and yet melodious bass voice regretfully, 'one must now expect this sort of thing, I suppose.'

M. Dubois was a tall and massive individual, exquisitely tailored, with the presence and dignity of a cardinal.

M. Pinaud had not the slightest difficulty in reading his thoughts.

The tone of his voice, in addition to his phrasing of the words, left no doubt whatever that in his opinion this character – now here, walking freely in these dignified and austere premises – in company with the dustman and the individual who came to read the meters, should have been relegated to the side door and the office upstairs, and never allowed inside his exclusive shop.

Well – if one must split hairs – the exclusive shop of Edmond Laroche. But who did all the work in it? What if the door should open again and a wealthy client unexpectedly appear?

M. Pinaud was completely unabashed.

'I am investigating the murder of Edmond Laroche,' he said quietly, replacing his wallet with his credentials in an inside pocket, 'And I would like to ask you a few questions.'

The muted and melodious voice immediately hardened and became aggressive.

'Then I suggest that you will be wasting your time, M'sieu Pinaud. As you no doubt already know, I shut and lock the safes down here at half-past five. M'sieu Laroche was in the habit of staying later. I was home soon after six o'clock, where I remained throughout the evening. If you would like witnesses – reputable and respected citizens – to confirm my statement, I will gladly let you have their names and addresses.'

There was a long silence, while M. Pinaud thought rapidly about what he should say next. After all, in the course of his long and interesting career, he had met many reputable and respected citizens who were quite capable of telling lies without the slightest hesitation for love or money or self-interest.

When at length he spoke, his voice was deceptively mild, ignoring the aggressive hostility of the remarks he had just heard.

'I am very pleased to hear what you have to say, M'sieu Dubois – for your sake. But the questions I was going to ask you were perhaps rather different.

'For example, what can you tell me about the private life and character of the late Edmond Laroche?'

For one brief moment sheer incredulity brought an almost human expression to the austere rigidity of those frozen and disapproving features in front of him.

27

Then he regained control, and it was as if the mask was donned again.

'The answer to that question, M'sieu Pinaud, is absolutely and definitely nothing,' he replied coldly. 'In the first place, such a thing is none of my business, and therefore I do not know. In the second place, even if I did, I would not tell you anything. A man's private life is his own concern.

'I can and will tell you that he was a good and fair employer, and that his unique and specialised knowledge commanded respect from all his employees.'

There was a long pause.

'I see.'

M. Pinaud regarded him thoughtfully.

'We can come back to this later. Another question, if you please, M'sieu Dubois.'

'Yes?'

'Who were these visitors M'sieu Laroche stayed late especially to see?'

This time the answer came without hesitation.

'To sell expensive and exclusive jewellery in a shop like this is always a delicate and lengthy business. With two or three important clients his whole day was occupied. Very often a lunch — from eleven until three — would be included.

'Yet there were other people, almost as important to his business, whom he had to see — people like travellers representing renowned and exclusive firms, dealers in precious stones, manufacturing goldsmiths and special clients. By these I mean that sometimes when he had a tricky valuation for insurance or probate he would prefer to see the owners of the jewellery in question personally.

'Since he was always so busy in the shop, he

adopted the very sensible habit of seeing these people by appointment in the evenings in his private office after this shop was closed. He was quite prepared to work very much harder than his staff. Which was to be expected, in view of the relative incomes he and they earned.'

M. Pinaud eyed the quality of the exquisite broad-cloth that draped the massive frame of M. Dubois, estimated swiftly what his tailor must have charged for that symphony in master-cutting, and came to the inescapable conclusion that the late Edmond Laroche must have been a very rich man indeed.

His features were impassive and completely expressionless as he spoke.

'Let us come back to my first question, M'sieu Dubois – the one that you refused so firmly and so emphatically to answer. The certainty and the conviction of your refusal made me wonder.

'Please do not misunderstand me – I am not blaming you or finding fault in any way. To encounter such loyalty is to me always a most refreshing and comforting experience. Perhaps because in my profession I encounter it so rarely. But often enough to prove my contention that human nature is an inexplicable and an astonishing thing. In a great and varied experience, I have found very few characters to be completely bad and without some redeeming features.'

M. Dubois stared at him aggressively.

'Why do you say bad?' he asked. 'Why do you assume, just because I refused to answer your question – which I considered impertinent and completely unjustified – that his character was necessarily bad?'

M. Pinaud drew himself up to his full and imposing height, and although his boots sank even deeper into

29

that yielding pile carpet, he still looked down at the tall and dignified figure of M. Dubois, up at whom so many wealthy and influential clients had gazed in awe and respect.

His reply came instantaneously with a devastating and ironic sarcasm that neither needed nor demanded an answer.

'Because, M'sieu Dubois, in my experience of bad characters – which I am sure you will concede is perhaps a little more extensive than yours – a man does not get murdered, stabbed in the back of his neck with malice aforethought, without a very good reason.'

He turned to leave the shop and spoke over his shoulder.

'If anyone else should feel inclined to question you about this brutal crime, M'sieu Dubois, I will instruct them to call on you here. Murder – if you will forgive me for pointing it out – is a far more serious business than selling jewels over a counter.'

Had it been possible, he would have slammed the front door shut. Perhaps with some justification. After all, he was only human – an ordinary man doing an arduous and exacting job – and the unctuous superiority of M. Dubois was not easy to accept.

But the late Edmond Laroche had spent thousands of francs on air-cylinders to ensure that the whole massive plate-glass contraption slid silently, effortlessly and sweetly into its oiled frame and grooves without the help of any human agency.

So that even this small pleasure he was denied.

He walked along to the side door and rang the bell, urgently and violently. He was fuming with impatience.

To be logical, if a man looked and acted like a cardinal, surely he would be far better employed in addressing a convocation of Monsignors rather than deliberately obstructing the honest efforts of a conscientious detective who was trying to do nothing more than to earn his living and find a murderer . . .

The office was small, but elegantly proportioned, with wide and lofty windows. The furniture was simple — a desk, a table with two chairs, a filing-cabinet and a bookcase — but all expensive and in good taste.

On the desk was a typewriter and on the table a large tall bowl of magnificent roses in an artistic and masterly arrangement. They varied from palest pink to the deep and almost glowing shade of crimson, the sizes, from bud to swelling open bloom, as beautifully arranged as their colours.

Louise de Granson, seated at her desk, was astonishingly beautiful, in spite of her high-bridged and aristocratic nose. Her hair was dark, simply and yet immaculately set, and the wide cool grey eyes looked at him not with contempt, for that would have denoted bad manners, which were unthinkable to one of her name, but with a marked and well-bred disdain.

M. Pinaud could read her thoughts as easily as if she had spoken them aloud.

This one was definitely not the type of man her father the Admiral would ever have invited to his house, but on the other hand it would be as well to remember that he was of the police. Even more—from the *Sûreté*. And everyone knows they have ferocious powers. Therefore it would be as well to be careful.

'Please sit down, M'sieu Pinaud,' she told him after

31

he had introduced himself. 'Although I am afraid you are wasting your time. There is very little that I can add to what I have already told the Inspector.'

Her voice was a deep and beautifully modulated contralto. He thought that with her presence and her appearance, and the background of a fine well-born family and an expensive education, she must have been just the type to deal with awkward and difficult clients, and therefore an invaluable asset to the late Edmond Laroche.

'Thank you,' he replied politely. 'What lovely flowers. I know I have to congratulate you – to a florist it becomes a matter of business and a profit, which is usually recognisable. Here I can see love, sympathy and understanding – and an artistic genius.'

She looked at him with a new interest, and for a brief and unforgettable moment the woman behind that armour of aristocratic reserve seemed to glow with an even greater beauty.

'Thank you,' she said quietly, with the very faintest emphasis on the second word. 'I bring them up from the country each week-end. I must say that you are a very unusual detective.'

He smiled.

'So they tell me. We do have ferocious powers, Mademoiselle, but there is hardly ever any need to use them and never to abuse them.'

He watched the blood surge to the wide pale brow and his smile deepened for another second. She was convinced now that he was not only a detective but also a mind-reader.

Then, abruptly, he became serious.

'I have heard about the two men who called here last night – you did not know them?'

'No. They must have been new clients. I know the voices of most of his trade suppliers.'

'And I have heard how you left Edmond Laroche alone to deal with his final visitor. But I am more interested in hearing what you can tell me about his character.'

She looked at him thoughtfully.

'Is that important?' she asked.

'Very important. It is all I have. No-one saw this visitor who may well have murdered him – unless someone else came afterwards. I must try to find out who it was.'

She hesitated and then seemed to make up her mind.

'I think I may be able to help you there. But first I will tell you what you want to know. Edmond Laroche was not a nice character. A brilliant business man – an expert gemmologist – but the morals of a monkey. I know his mother well. She is a wonderful old lady, but there was bad blood in the husband's family. His half-brother, Albert, whose father was killed in the war, is quite different.'

She paused and considered for a moment. M. Pinaud did not say anything.

'Now as to his visitor last night,' she continued. 'I was not there and so I do not know. But I think I ought to tell you that the night before a man named Henri Capet came to see him in his office. He is a Swiss watchmaker who repairs those marvellous singing birds in boxes we keep in stock.

'As I told the Inspector, I had instructions to leave this door ajar, in case I was needed. M'sieu Laroche never closed his. I did not usually see his visitors, as he always opened the door himself, nor

33

did I normally listen to their conversations, because they were not my business, and I always had enough work to do.

But some of this one I could not help overhearing. Capet's voice is distinctive and recognisable, and it was raised in anger. He was threatening M'sieu Laroche –'

'Why?' interrupted M. Pinaud.

'There was some trouble with Capet's daughter. She is pregnant. According to her father M'sieu Laroche was responsible.'

'Try to remember what he said. This is important,' he told her.

'Well – not his actual words, but their meaning was evident. The only thing he would accept would be for M'sieu Laroche to marry her. And he would expect an answer the following night.

'He said that no-one would have minded the girl being taken out for an evening, or even for a weekend at his home in the country. One would have assumed that Madame his mother was fully qualified to act as a chaperone – since she lives there. All this would have given great enjoyment to an artless and unsophisticated young girl. Therefore he did not object.'

Again she paused to consider. M. Pinaud waited, tensely but patiently.

'He said he did not object because he knew that M'sieu Laroche wished to show his gratitude for the very satisfactory repair-work he had been doing on the singing bird-boxes. He reminded him how he had heard in the trade that M'sieu Laroche was desperately trying to find someone fully capable and qualified to repair them. That was why he had come to the Rue de La Paix in the first place, especially to see him.

34

'With each sale of one of these boxes the firm made thousands of francs profit, and yet when something went wrong with one of them they had to rely on Henri Capet and his skill and willingness to work until late nearly every night. Clients who spent so much money were inclined to become somewhat upset and unreasonable when the bird no longer sang.

'It had been a very happy working arrangement, of mutual benefit to both of them. He would be sorry if it had to end in this way.'

Once more she paused. She had been staring at the roses, frowning slightly in the concentration of remembering. Now she looked at him and smiled.

'That is all," she added. 'Then he left.'

'And did you hear what Laroche replied?' he asked.

'No. His voice was quiet and not raised.'

'That is a great pity,' he said slowly, looking at her thoughtfully. Then he stood up.

'What you have told me is of great help, Mademoiselle de Granson,' he added. 'I am most grateful. If only you had also overheard his reply — that would have been invaluable. I am now going to look at the office next door —'

'You will not be able to do that,' she interrupted. 'The police locked the door and took the key.'

'I have it here,' he told her calmly, putting one hand in his pocket. 'I shall not be long. When I have finished, would you be kind enough to give me the address of this Henri Capet. If he did work for the firm, you will have a record in your files.'

'Of course.'

'Thank you. I will collect it on my way out when I give you back the key. We shall not need it any more.'

35

He thanked her once again and left her office to unlock the door of the adjoining room. This was an architectural duplicate of the one he had just left. It was furnished more simply and yet even more expensively.

There was a beautiful tapestry-inlaid table in the centre, with one matching chair behind it and another in front. The immense glass-fronted liqueur-cabinet took up most of the far wall. On the near and smaller wall hung a magnificent mirror, vast and rectangular, encased in a massive wooden frame, intricately carved and superbly ornate. By the opposite wall stood a telephone on a smaller table, flanked by two more chairs of the same pattern.

There was a huge and terrifying bloodstain on the thick and luxurious pile carpet in front of the cabinet, indicating where the body had fallen.

As he had expected from his conversations with M. le Chef and the doctor, M. Pinaud had not anticipated nor did he find any clues. The weapon had been withdrawn from the wound and taken away. With two other callers sitting at the table before the arrival of the murderer, it would have been a waste of time to look for fingerprints.

He contented himself with a glance of envious admiration at the quality and the quantity of the bottles inside the cabinet, remembered in time that he was on duty, and sternly admonished himself for not counting his blessings instead of harbouring thoughts of envy and admiration . . .

Of what use were all those exquisite bottles to Edmond Laroche, who was now nothing more than a bloodstain on a carpet?

THREE

'M'sieu Capet?'

'Yes.'

'My name is Pinaud. I am from the *Sûreté*. Here are my credentials.'

Capet hardly glanced at them.

'What is the matter that is of great importance?'

'Edmond Laroche, the jeweller, was murdered last night in his office. You knew him, I understand?'

'I did work for him, yes.'

The reply was given in a completely expressionless voice.

'I would like to ask you and your family a few questions.'

Capet opened the front door wider.

'Well, then – you had better come inside, M'sieu Pinaud. I apologise for my son's lack of good manners in keeping you waiting like this on the doorstep.'

'Thank you. Would it be possible to see you all separately?'

'Of course. If that is what you wish. We have a small room here.'

He opened a door behind him.

'I will tell them to be ready. Any special order?'

M. Pinaud stepped into a small study.

'You first, if you please. Then your son. Who else is there in the family?'

'My wife and daughter.'

'As they please.'

'Very well.'

Capet left the door open and went back down the passage to the living-room. He returned in a few moments, entered the study and shut the door. Then he gestured to a chair. M. Pinaud shook his head.

'I would prefer to stand, if you do not mind.'

'As you wish.'

Capet sat down himself.

'I am very tired,' he said. 'Now then, M'sieu Pinaud, what is all this about? Why are you here asking questions?'

'Because the night before last you were with him and threatened him.'

M. Pinaud's voice was impersonal and his features completely expressionless as he answered the question.

'And therefore I am your prime suspect?'

'Yes.'

Capet clasped his large and beautiful hands together under his chin and a very charming smile curved his lips.

'I see what you mean. I do not deny it. I lost my temper and must have been shouting loud enough for that frozen bitch of a secretary next door to have overheard me. But I did not kill him. Of that I can assure you.'

'Were you home at the usual time last night?'

'Yes. I had better tell you all about it. I repair — or I suppose I ought to say now that I used to repair those jewelled singing bird-boxes for him in the evenings, and I used to collect and deliver them once

38

or twice a week on my way home from work. If I was busy or delayed my family used to take them. That is how they all came to know him.'

'Did you see him last night?'

'No. I went there, as I told him I would, but I did not see him. There was no answer when I rang the bell.'

'What time was this?'

'I do not know exactly. It must have been at least six o'clock. I was late in leaving work.'

'Then at that time he may well have been already dead. That is why he could not come down to let you in.'

'Probably. I delivered one and collected two the night before. Last night I had to see him on a personal matter.'

'Your daughter?'

This time Capet did not smile. His eyes seemed to grow opaquely cold and hard. The long-nailed fingers tensed in a sudden spasmodic gesture.

'Yes. He made her pregnant.'

'There is no doubt?'

'Not in my mind.'

'What were you going to do?'

Capet hesitated.

'To be quite truthful with you, M'sieu Pinaud – I really do not know. I have never had any experience of this type of situation before. Trying to get a lawyer to sue for paternity – that I do know – is not easy. He would certainly need proof and evidence. There is none. And the costs would be astronomical.

'As everyone knows, witnesses can always be bribed. Laroche was an immensely wealthy man. I am not. I have to work twice as hard as any normal man

39

just in order to bring up my family decently and correctly. Laroche could easily have paid whatever fee a far more competent lawyer than mine would have asked.

'I had not even made up my mind when I went to see him the night before last. I have never had to think about such things before. Perhaps that is why I lost my temper and shouted.

'You must admit that I had some justification. The man was a godless fornicator who deserved to die.'

He unclasped his hands and laid them down, backs uppermost, long fingers in line, on the small table in front of his chair.

'Look – I am an artist and a craftsman. I take no credit for myself, since this is an indisputable fact. I am not responsible. This is something in my blood, which I have been blessed enough to inherit from my ancestors. The fact that I have recognised this miracle with humility and thankfulness and worked more than hard all my life in order to be worthy of this gift deserves perhaps some small credit to my name.

'The point I am trying to make, M'sieu Pinaud, is that the true artist and any dedicated craftsman must inevitably be a deeply religious man – otherwise in what can he believe? Who – and this word I spell with a capital letter – can give him the power and the inspiration to create and to use the miraculously inherited skill of his hands?'

Louise de Granson had told M. Pinaud that he was an unusual detective. She must have been right, because he did not ask another question. Instead he said quietly:

'I see exactly what you mean, M'sieu Capet.'

The watchmaker looked up from his hands, his

eyes shadowed and sombre.

'I am glad of that.'

'And what did you do then?'

'I told him – directly and forcefully – that he would have to marry her. There has never been a bastard in the Capet family and I was not going to allow him to father the first.'

'And his reply?'

'He laughed at me and insulted her.'

'And you? What did you do?'

'That was probably when I lost my temper and threatened him. I said I would call on the following evening for his answer. I was determined to bring some kind of pressure on him, even if I did not actually know what to do or how to do it.

'After that he seemed to relent – probably because of the expression he could see on my face. He said that he proposed to do exactly what he decided and wanted to do himself, and that he did not need any advice or assistance or instruction from other people in order to make up his own mind.'

'I see. Thank you for being so frank, M'sieu Capet. That will be all for the moment. Could I have a few words now with your son?'

'Of course. I will send him in.'

'Thank you.'

The boy Jean was tall for his age, powerfully built, and strangely mature and adult in his appearance. When he smiled, with an infectious and merry grin, that impression seemed to lose all its force and he became a schoolboy again.

M. Pinaud's voice was gentle, quiet and genuinely interested. He had that rare quality of sympathy which the young are the first to recognise and understand. Jean reacted at once, instinctively, as the young always do react when confronted with compassion, tolerance, sympathy and understanding.

'You are Jean, then — M'sieu Capet's son?'

'Yes, m'sieu.'

'You are still at school?'

'Yes. But I want to leave.'

'Why is that?'

'Because I want to be a watchmaker like him. He is the finest watchmaker in the world. He taught me how to use a screwdriver and tweezers and how to take a watch to pieces before I ever went to school.'

The love and admiration in his voice as he spoke seemed to surge and rise even above the intensity of the pride and emotion already in it.

Then it changed as he spoke about something entirely different, and he suddenly became a schoolboy again.

'And — besides — all the masters who are supposed to instruct me there are a lot of drips and half-wits. They treat you like a child — but none of them could organise a bunk-up in a brothel.'

'That I can well believe,' said M. Pinaud in a very grave and serious voice. 'It is an opinion I recognise from my own schooldays. But now what about Edmond Laroche?'

'Oh — I have met him. I sometimes collected urgent repairs on my way home from school if father was busy — the *Lycée* is not very far from the Rue de La Paix.'

'And what did you think of him?'

'Not much. He poked my sister and got her in the family way. Mind you, she probably asked for it —

42

she is completely dumb – a pea-brain in a seductive body – but naturally we all expected him to do something about it.'

'And did he?'

'No. Nothing. You have just seen my father, M'sieu Pinaud, so you know that he went there to reason with him. I do not know what he was told, but for me Laroche had no use. He just laughed when I told him about her and asked how anyone could prove that he had been responsible and not one of all the others who must have been up her.

'That was typical. That just shows. Who else would ever have dared to approach within a kilometre of mother's pet virgin? Only him, because he was a famous and celebrated jeweller and in addition a cash paying client of father.'

'And what did you do then?'

'Nothing at the time. I told you he had no use for me. He liked to make me wait at the bottom of the stairs until he condescended to come down and sign a receipt for what I had brought him – going home to fetch it specially after school, mind you – missing my tea and taking the Metro – because the repair was urgent. But when I got home, I might tell you, I thought a good deal.'

'About him?'

M. Pinaud's question followed as if it had been part of the same sentence.

'Yes.'

There was neither hesitation nor any expression in the boy's quick reply. His tone was flat and non-committal, and completely devoid of emotion. This was no longer a schoolboy.

M. Pinaud studied him thoughtfully for a long

43

moment. He obviously had no intention of amplifying his admission.

The silence seemed to surge on unbroken between them, borne on its own momentum, towards infinity. It was M. Pinaud who broke it.

'And what did you decide?'

The silence stayed between them. The boy's eyes met his own frankly, but as if from behind a veil, opaque, inscrutable, impenetrable.

'That would be telling,' he said slowly.

'You would not like to change your mind?' M. Pinaud asked him quietly.

'No.'

The reply as final and decisive.

'Did you go to the Rue de La Paix last night?'

'No. And even if I had I would still say no.'

For another long moment there was silence between them, as if their two minds were locked in opposition, destined to remain eternally apart, the boy astonishingly unafraid and mature, M. Pinaud studying him with interest and respect. This was the courage of youth — the courage that old age so mercilessly eroded. This was the self-confidence that bred men, this was a quality one had to admire . . .

Then suddenly the boy shivered, as if with cold, or the recollection of some terrible thing. Then he looked up and the infectious grin seemed to erase the maturity from his features.

'Look, M'sieu Pinaud — twice a week on the way home I call at the public library and bring home detective novels and murder mysteries. I read them in bed instead of learning the Latin verbs in my homework. There is no doubt as to which gives the better education. As you know, it is always the most unlikely

44

suspect who is guilty of the murder.

'If I were you, I would concentrate on finding out how many other girls Laroche poked and got into the family way. Then you can start to eliminate your suspects. That, I gather, is the classical method of deduction. But here you are wasting your time.'

'That,' M. Pinaud told him equably, 'is a matter of opinion. But there is one fact about which there can be no argument. It is always better to tell the truth.'

Something – some rare quality of sympathy, respect and understanding – seemed to strike a responsive chord in the boy facing him.

He hesitated, an irresolution strangely unnatural in his character, and then seemed suddenly to make up his mind.

'Perhaps you are right, M'sieu Pinaud – you are completely unlike any other detective I have read about in books. I will tell you the truth. I went home that night, shut myself up alone in my bedroom, and I thought for a long time. And I decided that a man like Laroche would be far better dead.'

He paused and waited. M. Pinaud did not say anything.

'But I did not kill him.'

Again he paused and again he waited, this time defiantly. Still M. Pinaud did not say anything. His features were completely expressionless.

Then, after a long silence, he turned and opened the door.

'Then, in that case,' he said quietly, 'I have no more questions. Would you please ask your mother or your sister to come in here.'

'Madame Capet?'

'Yes.'

'Please sit down.'

He looked with interest at her eyes, wise, tolerant and sad, and at her features, strong, fine-boned and beautiful, ravaged and strained with the aftermath of intolerable grief.

'Just relax, Madame. You look tense and nervous. There is no need to be either.'

His voice was kind, warm and sympathetic. She looked at him in astonishment as she sat down.

'But — but my husband says that he is suspect in a murder case, because he was heard threatening M'sieu Laroche —'

'All that can come later.'

'He said there would be questions —'

'There may be later. Anyone can answer questions. What I would like you to do now, Madame, is to tell me something about yourself and your family.'

She looked at him for a long moment and then visibly relaxed. A smile even touched the corners of the strong full mouth.

'You are a very persuasive man, M'sieu Pinaud. But I am afraid there is very little to tell. We have been a happy and united family — until recently — when —'

'Because of this trouble with your daughter?' he interrupted.

'Yes.'

Her reply was entirely devoid of expression. She did not enlarge on the subject, nor pursue it further.

'We have had our sorrows, like most married couples — I lost my second son when he was two. It was meningitis. You can imagine how much these two

46

mean to me. I would do anything for them.

'And we have had our share of happiness too. I have been married for many years to a good and hard-working man — no woman can ask for more.'

'Tell me more about him, Madame. He appears to be an exceptional character —'

The smile deepened slightly on her mouth.

'That is the correct word, M'sieu Pinaud. He is a superb and artistic craftsman — a watchmaker of exceptional and inherited skill. He spent ten years as an apprentice in the watchmaking school at Le Sentier in Switzerland — three years longer than usual — and when he left so that we could get married the master-watchmaker there, the great Louis-Elisé Piguet himself, told me that he was a genius.'

For a moment there was silence. M. Pinaud looked at her thoughtfully.

'Can a genius make a good husband, madame?' he asked.

'Why not — if his wife takes the trouble to give him patience, tolerance, love and understanding.'

'You mean the understanding of his work?'

'Naturally. That is the first duty and obligation of a wife married to such a man — to understand, to sympathise, to hearten and to encourage. To a man of this character, his work and his skill are really his whole life. Whatever comes occasionally to replace them can only be transient. He can know moments of great and rare happiness, because of the intensity of his feelings and the depths of his emotions, but his only true satisfaction can be in seeing, with humility and thankfulness, what his own hands have created.'

The quiet voice ceased, and this time the silence seemed to build up between them for a very long time

47

— not a silence of emptiness, not a mere absence of words, but something that seemed to surge around and between them in a torrent of emotion, a void of sound, but a surcharge of feeling . . .

When eventually M. Pinaud spoke, there was something in his voice that brought a flush to her brow.

'You must love him very greatly, Madame.'

Despite the flush, her eyes met his steadily and frankly.

'There is only one way to love, M'sieu Pinaud.'

'I quite agree. How few people seem to realise it.'

For a while they remained there, each one silent in thought. Then he changed his position and the spell was broken.

'Now tell me about your daughter, Madame,' he said quietly. His voice was still gentle, kind and sympathetic.

Afterwards, she remembered everything she had said, even the very words she had chosen and used, and she had the strange impression that they had never really been spoken of her own volition, but drawn out of her by that gentle and sympathetic kindness and the extraordinary magnetism of his unique personality.

'There is not very much to tell,' she began quietly. 'An old tale about a young and beautiful and foolish girl who has got herself into trouble, as so many others have done before her, and no doubt will do so often again.

'And about an unscrupulous man with no conscience and too much money to spend on a simple-minded girl who believed everything he promised and said. I do not think he would ever have married her even if he had lived. He was not the marrying type. This we realise now — now that it is too late.

'She met him one evening for the first time when my husband asked her to deliver an urgent repair. She was completely fascinated by his personality. He suggested a quick drink to compensate for her trouble, opened his cabinet and gave her a very modest glass of the finest sherry she had ever tasted. She talked about it for days, because it was poured from a decanter and she did not have enough confidence in herself to ask him what it was.

'His manner was perfectly correct, courteous and charming, his behaviour exemplary. He sent her home quickly in a taxi and hoped politely that he would have another urgent repair as soon as possible.

'Naturally she asked her father if she could deliver the next one when it was ready. We saw no reason to refuse, even if on her part it was an infatuation. This man was a wealthy bachelor, a valued client of my husband, who paid his debts promptly and enjoyed a reputation second to none in the jewellery trade.

'This time it was a longer drink, again upstairs in his office, and an even longer talk. All very correct and business-like. Then, a few days later, a dinner-dance at a very respectable night-club, with our permission and consent, from which she was driven home at a fitting and respectable time in his car.

'And so one thing led to another, and finally it was a week-end in the country. His mother has a huge old house somewhere in the heart of the south. We understood that Yvonne would be staying there with her. What we did not know was that he had had part of it rebuilt as a completely self-contained flat.

'We did not interfere. We were wrong. We see that now — now that it is of no use. But how can we be blamed? Where are the parents who do not hope and pray for a happy and successful marriage for their only daughter?

'Here was a rich, proud and celebrated bachelor, the part owner of one of the most exclusive jewellers in the Rue de La Paix, going out of his way to court our child Yvonne — just the type of man, we thought, who might prefer — from all the prospective and eligible daughters eager and available — a simple and unsophisticated girl so much younger than he was himself.'

The quiet voice ceased, smothered by the memories of what might have been. He neither spoke nor moved, and felt emotion as he watched the courage of her smile.

'It is an old story,' she went on, 'and a sad one. With children you give hostages to fortune and heart-break to yourself —'

'And yet they are worth both — infinitely worth while,' he interrupted her gently. And the kindness and compassion in his voice brought the tears to obliterate her smile.

'I believe you, M'sieu Pinaud,' she replied slowly. 'But that is something we are both finding very hard to accept these days.'

He bent forward from his massive and impressive height and took her right hand in both of his. His clasp was warm and reassuring, the tenderness of his powerful fingers a benediction.

'Have courage, Madame,' he said quietly. 'There is always a way out. You and I — we shall find one. I have no more questions. But I would like to see Yvonne herself for a few moments, if you would be kind enough to tell her.'

'Please sit down, Mademoiselle Capet.'

'Thank you.'

Her civility was barely gracious.

'I would like to ask you a few questions.'

'Why? If I am pregnant – what concern is that of yours?'

Her tone was aggressive and even offensive, her eyes veiled and hostile. His voice did not have the slightest change of expression as he answered.

'More perhaps than you think.'

'My pregnancy has nothing to do with you.'

'It might have.'

'Why?'

He paused for quite a while, considering, deep in thought. Then, when he spoke, his voice was hard and cold, with a merciless and threatening edge to it that made her shiver.

'Look, Mademoiselle Capet, I am a detective officially investigating a murder – the murder of the man who would have fathered your child. I have neither the time nor the inclination to respect your maidenly and outraged dignity nor to put up with any more of your childish nonsense.

'All the remarks, suggestions and innuendos you may have heard and which have obviously upset you have nothing to do with me. I am concerned only with facts. These will give me information.'

Again he paused, and when he spoke again she stared at him in amazement, hardly able to believe that this was the same man speaking with the same voice that had just terrified her.

Now his tone was gentle, kind and sympathetic, willing and inducing her confidence, assuring her of his trust, his goodwill and his understanding.

'Just tell me, in your own words, exactly what happened. By that I mean when it all started and how it went on. It should not be difficult. It will do you good to talk about it.'

He waited without speaking while she sat there, feeling all the barriers of her reserve, indignation and hostility breaking down like matchwood before the genuine warmth and the obvious honesty of his approach.

She began with a slow hesitation as if uncertain what to say, but soon the words came rapidly, eagerly and gladly, reaching out gratefully in acceptance of his sympathetic understanding as she described the events that had so miraculously changed and so dramatically transformed her whole life during the past few months.

'It is not easy to put into words — at first it was like entering into a fairyland, an entirely different world I never knew existed. What I am trying to say it that there have never been very many opportunities to go out from this home. My parents were always too strict. And now they are far too busy. There is always too much work waiting to be done. Until I med Edmond I had led a very quiet and sheltered life.

'He asked me into his office for a drink that first time when I took him one of father's urgent repairs. He was so kind and courteous and charming — he made me feel like a great lady or a queen. My brother Jean makes me feel like a half-wit. With Edmond I knew that I was really somebody — a person who counted, a girl who mattered. And right from that first moment we were so completely in a sympathetic accord — it was unbelievable.

'Then dinner and dancing at a night-club. All very

respectable. Then the theatre and concerts. And always back home at the correct time. No frantic parents. No complications. No doubts. Just a dream-world of enchantment and happiness.

'And he was always so kind and attentive – so generous. He had such gracious and cultured manners, and so much compelling authority when talking or giving orders to others – he made all the boys and young men I have ever known seem awkward and immature.

'And then those week-ends in the country, at his mother's *Château* near Valoisin in Touraine – those were days of magic I shall never forget.'

She paused and drew in her breath in a long sobbing gasp.

'I have no regrets for what has happened,' she continued, with the slow tears now welling up and brimming over her eyes. 'In spite of all my father's doubts and torments and anxieties and my mother's agonies – I have no regrets. Only one, perhaps – that he is dead. I have had more than my share of happiness – and no-one can ever take that away.'

The eager and excited words died into a silence which he was careful not to break.

She sat there on the small chair, an awkward, pathetic and yet somehow splendidly dignified figure in her complete acceptance of the inevitable, the slow tears now following each other down her cheeks, her hands clasped fiercely in her lap.

And behind the tears he imagined he could see a glow of satisfaction as she remembered the happiness that once – even though briefly – had given life and such glorious substance to her dream . . .

FOUR

He unlocked his car, got in, started the engine and drove away from the flat.

He normally drove fast. Now he accelerated and tried to drive even faster, because he knew that if he really concentrated on what he was doing he could be home in time to participate in the uproarious fun of his young daughters' bath, in which wet, wasteful and riotous ritual he always took a supreme delight.

He noticed with annoyance and exasperation that the steering felt heavy and sluggish, which did not help his efforts.

Just like his mind, he reflected moodily as he swung out to pass a cruising taxi and stayed out on the wrong side of the road, which was clear, to include a few private cars with somnolent drivers in the same operation.

How could any of these respectable family types he had just questioned be possibly connected with murder? He felt that he had been wasting his time. And yet it was the only lead he had. Even though he was young, his experience was sufficient to confirm that murderers very often turned out to be the most unlikely people.

The enormous lorry in front of him had twelve

wheels and was transporting a vast load of steel girders at an illegal speed along the main city thoroughfare.

The road ahead curved, but was clear. He changed down, stamped the accelerator to the floor and swung out to pass the whole gigantic contraption in the one same and swift movement.

Then three things happened simultaneously.

His two front tyres blew out with an indescribable and deafening noise, the steering-wheel turned in his hands but had no functional effect and the front of his car, in that wild surge of acceleration, crashed into the back of the lorry.

Considering the excessive speed at which he had been travelling, the lorry driver — a competent type like most of his kind — put up a very creditable performance in stopping his load, even though he was considerably helped by the dead weight of the wrecked car, now inextricably tangled with the ends of some of the protruding steel girders.

He climbed out and dropped down from the high cab with an easy and cat-like grace, a huge black-bearded individual clad in jeans and a blue shirt. Then he walked slowly down the side of his immense lorry.

M. Pinaud had been saved from injury by his safety-belt. He snapped it free and was thankful to find that the door had not jammed although the damage seemed mainly to the front of the car. He opened it quickly and got out.

But he had no time to survey the scene, for the lorry driver was now standing beside him and talking in a loud, aggressive and fantastically powerful voice. His comments were caustic, pithy and apt, and pungent with a great and pitying contempt.

'All I am trying to do is to earn an honest living

by taking a load of steel girders to Billancourt. Only an idiot, a fanatic or a Communist would try to stop me. And if he wanted to do that – and were not mentally deficient – he would obviously drive the other way and steer into me head-on. In that manner he might kill or maim me, and very probably achieve his objective by setting the whole bloody issue on fire, with all that diesel oil pouring out on to a hot exhaust-pipe.'

All this had been exhaled as a torrent of eloquence in practically one breath. Now he paused to refill his depleted lungs. But as M. Pinaud opened his mouth to reply he started again.

'Look at your car, M'sieu – just look at the front of it. What could you hope to achieve by driving – as you did – into the back of my lorry? By steering into reinforced iron bars, specially designed to take the weight of steel girders? They must have taught you at school – you look an intelligent type – that these do not buckle or bend.'

For the second time he paused, but once again M. Pinaud realised that he was wasting his time in trying to speak. After one deep and quick gulp of air, that amazing powerful voice roared on with unabated vigour.

'Hey, m'sieu – you look a bit green. Have some of this.'

From the inside of his blue shirt he produced a pocket-flask, and with a dexterous and powerful twist of his huge and hairy fingers levered up the hinged cap.

'It is not surprising that you look green. There is nothing more upsetting than having to watch the front of your car being bashed in – and nothing more comforting than a drop of *kirsch* to warm your insides afterwards. Go on – take a good swig. You look as though you need it.'

'Thank you. I appreciate your kindness.'

He took a deep swallow from the flask, and felt immediately a sensation as if the top of his head had been blown off. Beneath the diabolical strength of the distillation he could definitely taste the crisp tenderness and tangy juiciness of the superb cherries that had been used for the fermentation.

'Thank you once again. This is a remarkable liqueur – the best *kirsch* I have ever tasted.'

'You are welcome. It ought to be. My brother makes it, and he has had forty years' experience. He farms over the border in Switzerland, in the Canton de Vaud, where they not only make fine watches but have some considerable experience in these far more important matters.

'I drink with you in sympathy, because I know just how you feel. I myself once owned a car. My heart bleeds for you.'

With a bleeding heart he might not talk so much. M. Pinaud felt that it was time he justified himself.

'May I say here and now and explain that all this was in no way my own fault. I am neither an idiot, nor a fanatic, nor yet a Communist. I had a blow-out on both of my front tyres and the car did not respond to the steering.'

'Right. Fair enough. That can happen to anyone. Now I understand. As I said before – you look an intelligent type to me. Everything is in order and going well. Have another drink.'

Warmed, comforted and inspired by the contents of that remarkable flask, which they soon finished between them, they were busily and amicably engaged in exchanging the addresses and telephone numbers of their respective insurance companies when the first inevitable spectators arrived.

'This is the second one I have seen, Gustave. My sister-in-law's cousin hit a lorry as well last week. Only he hit it in the front. Took his head off as clean as a whistle. They were able to find it on the back floor, because fortunately the lorry was empty. And the blood — you should have seen the blood — like a bath —'

'Yes, I can well imagine. I too saw one hit the front of a lorry — only that one had sixteen wheels. This one has only twelve.'

'Why this type should have chosen to ram himself up the back of a lorry is beyond my comprehension. What on earth was he trying to achieve?'

'They had to use oxy-acetylene torches to get the bodies out. Luckily there was a parking-place just opposite — it kept the children quiet for over an hour just watching them —'

'Any normal and sane government would have passed legislation long ago to ban monstrosities like this from the inner city. I call it an absolute disgrace. We have architectural treasures here that people come from all over the world to admire — their foundations were never designed to withstand such vibration and stress. What will happen when they start to fall down in a few years' time?'

'The husband of Hortense used to drive one of exactly the same type. He is now in a wheel-chair. Nothing left below the waist. Only half a man. A dog ran out in front of him and he tried to avoid it. Hit the parapet of the bridge —'

'Now this one, Theophile, must obviously have been drunk — to drive like that into the back of a lorry. Would any sober man attempt such a thing? The lorry had back lights. The car presumably was manufactured with brakes. It stands to reason —'

'I agree with you, Emil — entirely. Of course, some people do not show it. I had a schoolmaster who used to drink a half-bottle of brandy every day after lunch. No-one even suspected it until he was packed off in disgrace. But I tell you this, Emil — his afternoon classes in mediaeval history were a joy and an inspiration to everyone. He could make the very people come alive — you could see them as he spoke — pleading, declaiming, acting and posturing — they were not only historical names. They were something more — much more. They were living people.'

The arrival of a police-car — by terminating M. Pinaud's philosophical reflections on the complexity of human nature — diminished their audience to two, as he and his new friend the lorry driver began to explain the situation.

The garage-man was sympathetic, courteous and intelligent. He was also clad in an immaculate white coat, of which M. Pinaud approved.

As he spoke he wiped his hands meticulously on a clean piece of waste.

'In answer to your question, m'sieu — which I find both strange and interesting — the trouble might well have been started by the skilful application of a short thin knife — a very sharp one, mind you — just penetrating far enough between the treads to allow the air to start to escape slowly as soon as you drove away. If you normally drive fast — and from the look of your car now there can be little argument about that — then the rest would not take long.

'I say strange and interesting advisedly, because I know that you gentlemen in your daily work are compelled to meet the most extraordinary characters.'

He had been very impressed by the *Sûretés* card. Now he regarded M. Pinaud with grave concern.

'Mind you — this is only my opinion, m'sieu. There is no proof. There never will be any proof. Both your front tyres are now in shreds.'

'Yes. I see what you mean,' said M. Pinaud thoughtfully.

While he had been with the mother and the daughter, either the father or the son could easily have gone downstairs to his car. They both had the skill and the manual dexterity necessary.

But why? What was the point? If anything had happened to him, someone else would have taken over. Had it been an act of panic — the blind instinct of self-preservation? Or had it been to protect the other two — an act of consequence they could not have done themselves?

He turned his thoughts from speculation to the present and addressed the garage-man briskly.

'Well — it looks like a very complicated repair. The sooner you start it the better. I would be grateful if you would undertake it for me.'

The garage-man looked doubtful.

'I would prefer — and it would be more fitting — to send you a written estimate, m'sieu. As you say, this is not a simple matter. Two new front tyres, probably new wheels and brake-drums, new radiator, head, side, fog and indicator lamps, hood, wings, panels, battery, fan, hose-pipes, windscreen, dynamo, coil, battery, petrol-pump, distributor, carburettor, brake-cylinder —'

M. Pinaud held up his hand and smiled as he interrupted.

'There is no need to go on — I can see and admire your competence, m'sieu. And there is no need to send an estimate — just get the work done as soon as possible. Our insurance will pay your bill. I am sure you will make a good job of it.'

His smile was infectious. The garage-man cheered up visibly. One did not welcome such clients every day. They parted with mutual expressions of esteem and goodwill.

The following morning M. le Chef was not so pleased. He frowned at his eminent detective.

That was the trouble with human nature — give a man some small success, or even — to be fair — several large and outstanding triumphs, and immediately they went to his head. Then he had to be cut down to size. Although, in all fairness to this one, he had never noticed any of these symptoms before.

With all his faults, he was essentially a fair man, and therefore when he spoke his remark was not as severe as his frown.

'I have always told you, Pinaud, that you drive too fast. Some of these trips you make are hard to believe.'

It did not seem an opportune moment to bring up the subject of the urgency of his daughters' bath, and so M. Pinaud kept his features expressionless as he replied.

'I was on duty, m'sieu. I wanted to get home as soon as possible in order to sort out my impressions

61

of this Capet family. The faster I drove the more time I would have to think.'

'Granted. I am not blaming you for the accident — no-one can cope with blown-out tyres. But if you had been driving at a reasonable speed, the damage would not have been so extensive, nor so costly.'

'Yes, m'sieu. But the insurance will pay.'

'And we lose our bonus.'

His reply, quite unconsciously, was tinged with venom.

Then he relented. After all, the fame of this one's exploits had already reached the other side of the Atlantic. It would not do to discourage him.

'Well,' he continued in a more reasonable tone, 'never mind now. It is all done and finished. Draw another car from the pool on your way out. Now then, how are you getting on with these Capets? Did you have any time to think about them?'

'No, m'sieu. I did not. I was compelled to waste most of my evening talking to the police and a garage-man. I have four suspects, but no proof. A short thin knife, of the kitchen pattern, very sharp, was probably the murder weapon. There was bound to be a knife of this type in such a household. If there was, you can be sure it is no longer there for any comparisons to be made with the wound.

Any one of them could have done it. They all had provocation and justification.'

'Why?'

'The daughter is pregnant by Laroche, who refused to marry her. Either she, the mother or the son could have killed him. And the father was heard threatening him the night before.'

'Did you look for the knife?'

'No, m'sieu.'

'Why not?'

'I had no search-warrant. This was only a preliminary investigation, based on the information Louise de Granson gave me.'

'You can get one now.'

'Too late. It will no longer be there, especially if someone used it on my front tyres.'

'You think that was the cause of your accident?'

'I really do not know. I interviewed them separately, one at a time. I cannot see the mother or the daughter being able to do something like that, but either the father or the son would have known how.'

'But why? What was the point? Even if they had killed you, I would have sent someone else. That would have been no solution for them.'

'I do not know that either. I was thinking about it in the garage. Perhaps panic. Perhaps just to gain time. Maybe with some mistaken idea of protecting the women.'

'That could be. People do strange things when they are frightened.'

'Agreed.'

There was a short silence. Then M. Pinaud hesitated before he spoke, slowly and thoughtfully.

'Although – it is strange – they did not give me the impression of being either frightened or guilty people. They seemed so – so honest – so forthright – a normal hard-working family to whom something unexpected and terrible had happened. Their reactions were typical, their answers in keeping with the situation as they saw it.'

M. le Chef considered for a long moment.

'Yes, Pinaud,' he said at last. 'I see what you mean.

63

But I do not have to tell you that all these normal and apparently reasonable people are just the ones who react the most violently to the unexpected – for the simple reason that its impact on their ordered lives is so much the greater, in that hitherto it has been unknown.'

There were no flies on the old bastard, M. Pinaud thought morosely, or else he would not be where he was now, sitting on his backside as head of the *Sûreté*, drawing and spending an enormous salary while others did all the work and risked their lives for a mere pittance. The mere fact that he was making an impossible case even harder in no way detracted from the sound common sense of his observations.

'You are quite right, m'sieu,' he said civilly. 'This is going to be a hard one. I will keep in touch and let you know what happens.'

'Good. You do that.'

Suddenly a charming and friendly smile transfigured the ruthless and ascetic mouth.

'And take care, Pinaud. Try not to drive so fast.'

FIVE

He had been conducted by an immaculate and fault-lessly clothed manservant through the endless rooms and corridors of the beautiful old *Château* into this gracious and lovely room at the back, with its lofty windows facing out on to a vast old-world garden.

'This gentleman is M'sieu Pinaud, from the *Sûreté*, madame,' the manservant intoned, his voice as expressionless as his features were impassive. 'His credentials would appear to be completely in order.'

He looked with interest at the lady seated in a high wing-chair beside the table.

'Madame Laroche?'

'Yes. What is it?'

Her voice was arrogant, imperious and self-assured. In the dominant and lined features he imagined he could recognise something of the fierce cruelty of an eagle's stare.

'Thank you, Charles. That will be all.'

The words were a dismissal.

'Thank you, madame.'

He went out, shutting the tall linen-fold door without a sound.

'My name is Pinaud. I represent the *Sûreté*.'

'Well — what has that to do with me?'

'I am investigating the murder of your son Edmond Laroche.'

She reminded him of a portrait he had once seen of a Roman Emperor seated on his Imperial throne. Here were the fine, broad and intelligent forehead and the same ruthless and dominant nose.

But there the resemblance ended. This was a woman's mouth, soft and full-lipped, with a rounded and feminine chin. And the dress, cut in the same flowing and full lines as a robe, was not white with the Imperial purple, but of the deepest black.

'Have you been specifically asked or ordered to come here and do this?'

'No, madame.'

'Then let me tell you that I regard your intrusion and your present here as an intolerable impertinence. You will leave at once.'

'No, madame.'

'What do you mean?'

'Murder is our business. That is why I am here. That is why I will not leave.'

Their glances locked and held, rigid, tense and unyielding. It seemed to his vivid imagination that the moment lasted an eternity. They were doomed to remain apart forever.

He remained standing. He had not been offered a chair.

Then she turned her head and reached out one hand. From the table she took up a small gold box, encrusted with an exquisite pattern of crescent-cut diamonds. She moved a slide, the oval lid opened and a tiny feathered bird spring up, pivoted on its wheel and began to sing.

As the miniature beak opened and closed she

watched him attentively, but now with an entirely different glance, thoughtfully and appraisingly.

But this he did not see. His rapt and fascinated stare was entirely concentrated on the singing bird, standing and watching and listening with a complete and absorbed interest. In his whole life he had never seen anything like this before.

The song ended. The bird folded down and the lid snapped shut. It was Madame Laroche who spoke first, with all the same arrogance in her tone.

'I do not intend – nor am I compelled – to have any unpleasantness here, M'sieu Pinaud.'

His reply came without the slightest hesitation.

'Murder happens to be a very unpleasant thing, madame.'

'So I believe. But it has nothing to do with me here in this house. My son was murdered in Paris. He made his bed. He was the one to lie in it.'

He looked at her with honest incredulity.

'Is that all you can say?'

'Of course not. But it is all I am saying to you.'

She paused for a moment and then added:

'Except, perhaps, to point out that I find your overbearing manner extremely insolent.'

He contemplated her for a long moment. Then, without any change of expression, he reached into his hip-pocket and took out his handcuffs.

This woman, with her in-bred assumption that the whole country was her own private domain and all the people therein her servants, was beginning to get on his nerves.

His voice, in its quiet, cold and menacing tones when he spoke, frightened her – she who had never known fear in her life.

'Madame Laroche,' he said, deliberately and emphatically, 'by virtue of my employment I have the authority to lock these handcuffs on your wrists and take you now to your police station here in Valoisin on a charge of obstructing justice and —'

'You must be mad —'

The whispered interruption was malignant in the intensity of its hate.

'On the contrary, madame. I am sane, qualified and I believe competent within my own authority. Which is the authority of the state. Which is far greater than that of individuals by the name of Laroche. You are dealing with murder, madame — not with social caste or etiquette or good manners.'

'How dare you?'

With one sudden movement — shocking in its savage violence — she snatched up the bird-box from the table and flung it on the floor.

He did not even look down. His complete ignoring of her display of wilful temper made his condemnation of her action all the more effective, even in some indefinable way — as he continued to stand there impassively — terrifying to her.

Instead he answered her question, his voice once again without inflection.

'It is not a matter of daring, madame. I am doing my duty and earning my salary.'

'You might well find yourself soon without either, M'sieu Pinaud.'

He studied her for a long moment, his eyes unfathomable.

'I have heard threats before, madame,' he told her quietly.

'And what have you done?'

'I ignore them.'

Then he looked down. The box had fallen on its side, the spring lid shattered and separate, the bird on its wing, apart and off its pivot, incongruously tiny and pathetic.

'That was one of the most beautiful and fascinating things I have ever seen in my life,' he said, and the warmth and intensity of emotion in his voice made him seem a different person. 'How could you bring yourself to destroy it in a fit of childish and wanton temper —'

She waved her hand imperiously as she interrupted him.

'Nonsense. That is nothing. It was a birthday present from Edmond, and he is dead. There is a man in Paris called Capet who repairs them.'

Then she clasped her hands together, placed them under her chin and looked at him very thoughtfully for a long moment, her hooded eyes completely expressionless.

When she spoke her voice was entirely different — courteous, charming and pleasant.

'Would you be kind enough to take a chair, M'sieu Pinaud — and to accept my apologies for not having offered it before. Has anyone ever told you that you are a most unusual detective?'

'Thank you.'

He sat down and smiled, and the strong brooding lines of his features were transfigured.

'I believe that thanks to the untiring efforts of my faithful chronicler certain of the more enlightened publishers are at last beginning to form a school of thought which might confirm that opinion. For myself, I do not know.'

Again she seemed to think for a long moment before she spoke.

'Tell me, M'sieu Pinaud – why exactly are you here?'

There was no hesitation in his reply.

'To find out all I can about your son's character and background.'

'Why?'

'In the hope that something may give me a clue concerning his murder. I intend to find out who killed him.'

'But why is the finding out so important? Edmond is dead. Let him lie in peace. Perhaps he is better dead. Let the matter end.'

'No, madame. That is the one thing which is completely impossible.'

The conviction in his voice as he continued to speak was final.

'This is my work, my ambition and my self-respect. I intend to go on trying. Nothing will stop me until I have found out the truth.'

He spoke, quite unconsciously, with an impassioned sincerity that was strangely moving. Once more the hooded and unfathomable eyes contemplated him for some time.

'There are occasions when it is better to leave things are they are, M'sieu Pinaud.'

'No, madame. Never when murder is concerned.'

'It might not have been murder, but execution. Who is to judge?'

Now it was his turn to study her, very carefully and thoughtfully, but her features were expressionless, her eyes dark and impenetrable pools of thought.

'Not you or I, madame. I have had experience of cases which make me believe that there is a higher judge, whose decision is final. But I have my duty. I will find out the truth.'

When he had said this she did not answer for some time. Then, suddenly, she seemed to come to a decision. Abruptly, she stood up.

As he started to rise from his own chair she waved him back.

'Very well. I will tell you what you want to know. May I offer you some refreshment, M'sieu Pinaud? And I hope you will stay to dinner this evening. We are a long way from Paris, and you must have driven both fast and far. I am beholden to a tradition of hospitality in this house which dates from the days when it was built as a monastery. There are guest-rooms and you can return in the morning.'

This time he not only started to get out of his chair, but stood up in spite of her imperiously waving hand.

'I am sorry, madame,' he replied quietly, 'but in spite of the kindness and the courtesy of both your invitations, I am afraid that the answer must be no.'

She looked at him in open wonder, this time taking no pains to conceal the genuine astonishment she obviously felt that a lowly species such as a detective from the *Sûreté* should have the unwonted temerity to refuse the generosity of such an offer.

'But why? What can be your reason?'

'I am on duty. I have said that I am sorry.'

She saw that his mind was made up, his purpose inflexible. And so with that amazing self-command and co-ordination which characterised her every decision and movement she immediately accepted the situation and sat down once again in her chair.

71

'Very well. Then listen carefully. I shall not repeat myself.'

'You have all my attention, madame,' he told her gravely.

Now, although her eyes never left his, he knew that she no longer saw him. They were dark with memory, opaque with thoughts from the past.

'We — that is, my family — have lived in this house since it ceased to be a monastery in the twelfth century. My maiden name was Valois. One branch became the Kings of France. We have our pride.

'But Edmond was always a problem child, a debased character, a disgrace to our name and a shame to that pride. Mind you, I am the first to admit that it was probably my own fault. I made an unfortunate mistake. I married a second time into bad blood.'

'Edmond's father?'

'Yes.'

She paused for a moment, but when she continued to speak there was not the slightest change in the inflection of her voice.

'Mercifully, he had enough good sense to kill himself. But not soon enough. If only he had done so before I was fool enough to marry him, my life would have been far less complicated. And Edmond might have suffered less. When he was young and wild there was no control. I did what I could. I did my best. But a boy needs a father. Especially a boy like Edmond and the man he grew up to be.

'I tried. I established two of his bastards in the village, when they grew up, one in a garage and one on a farm. Both the mothers died in childbirth. They were young schoolgirls who got frightened and ran

72

away when it was too late, instead of coming to me and asking for help and advice. I would like you to believe that I tried. But it was of no use.'

Again she paused, while the horror of what she had said seemed to quiver and surge with a life of its own in the still and silent air. M. Pinaud did not say anything. He stood there in front of her, his features impassive, waiting for her to continue.

'Recently he started going out with a poor type, Capet's daughter. Not a common type — after all, some Capets too were once the Kings of France — but an ignorant one. There was never enough money, I believe, for her to have been brought up and educated in the correct way. That was no fault of hers.

'He took her out, apparently, to night-clubs, dance-halls, dinners and theatres in town. Enough to completely infatuate her. He did this deliberately. He only wanted one thing. He was that type of man.

'Then he brought her home here. He has — he had his own suite of rooms, in which he did what he liked. I could not control him.

'For her I have neither blame nor censure. She was obviously in love with him. And when young girls are in love they do strange things.'

Then her voice changed and became animated.

'What a contrast to his secretary, Louise de Granson. Ah — there is a lady. There is one who was properly and correctly brought up. When he invited her here she insisted on having a room next to mine, and left her door wide-open all night.

'Our minds were completely in accord. In the best families there are certain things which are done, and others which are never done. She was his newly engaged secretary, here in this house to meet with my approval, since I have a considerable amount of money invested in that shop. And she knew the right way in which to get that approval.'

She paused and nodded her head in complete satisfaction.

'For Edmond,' she continued, 'I no longer have any feelings at all. He took a mother's great love and turned it into something like hatred a long time ago. And now he is dead. All I ask is to be left in peace and in the hope that this absurd investigation will not go on.'

'I am afraid that is quite impossible, madame,' he said quietly.

She considered him thoughtfully for a long moment. 'We shall see.'

Her voice was as quiet as his. He had the strange impression that she was speaking, not to him, but to herself. He decided that the best thing to do would be to ignore her remark.

'Would there have been any chance, madame,' he asked her, 'that your son Edmond reciprocated her feelings and genuinely fell in love with this girl?'

There was no hesitation in her reply.

'I do not know. From the day he grew to manhood he was a stranger to me – a complete stranger – an alien. To me – his own mother.'

Then, suddenly and surprisingly, the tears came to her eyes – so shockingly out of keeping with that implacable strength and determination of character which had so impressed him that his own eyes misted as he watched them brim and overflow and course down the strong and arrogant lines of her cheeks.

SIX

He drove his car down the straight and narrow main street of the village of Valoisin until he came to the garage.

He glanced at the guage. His tank was nearly empty. He turned the car off the road into the small forecourt which enclosed the one petrol-pump, switched off the engine and got out.

There was no-one in the office. The forecourt was deserted.

At the far end he saw an immense car with an unbelievably long bonnet. The chassis had been fitted by a master coach-builder with a body that had once been known as a *sedanca de ville*, which fact alone relegated the car automatically to a place of honour in any museum.

A tall young man, clad in overalls, was stooping down on the near side, polishing the coachwork assiduously with a velvet pad.

M. Pinaud had always been interested in old cars. This one, he knew at once, was one in a thousand. He walked across the forecourt. The young man straightened and turned at the sound of his footsteps.

M. Pinaud stopped in sheer astonishment. He wondered if he was seeing a ghost — the ghost of the man who now lay, sightless and unseeing, on a tray in a morgue in Paris.

The likeness was extraordinary. Here were the same bone-structure, the same contour of jaw, the same fleshy and arrogant features, younger and firmer, unravaged by time, unsullied by evil living. Here was Edmond Laroche as he might once have been, young, virile and handsome.

But nothing of his astonishment showed on M. Pinaud's features. Even as he remembered Madame Laroche's recent words about the two bastards she had established, one in a garage and one on a farm, his only expression was one of excited and enthusiastic interest. Having stopped, he remained where he was.

'I say – what a car. This is the father and mother of all cars. Would you mind very much if I had a look at it?'

The rapture in his voice was infectious. The young man smiled. He had a charming smile. His eyes were clear, shining and intense. This car was nearly always outside in good weather, but so many motorists stopped for petrol and drove off again without a second glance, always busy with their own thoughts, always in a hurry to look after their own affairs. This sounded like a man after his own heart.

'Of course not, m'sieu. But do you want petrol?'

'Yes – would you please fill the tank. But there is no hurry for that. May I leave the car here in your forecourt while I have something to eat?'

'Anywhere you like – provided it is away from the pump.'

'Of course. Thank you. Is there a good *café* near?'

'You passed it as you came in. About three buildings away, next to the bank. The Eight Bells. The food is more than good — it is superb.'

'Thank you.'

He walked nearer.

'May I see the engine?'

'Of course.'

The young man opened the front door and released the catch. Then he came back, lifted the immense bonnet which swung up without effort on its own counter-weights. There was no supporting rod. It was not necessary.

'Now that,' said M. Pinaud reverently, 'that is what I call an engine.'

'I should think so,' the young man replied. 'Six cylinders in line. Nine litres. This one was made when the two brothers first started at Billancourt. Look at the lines — the cleanness and the simplicity — the proportion and the grace —'

'Beautiful,' interrupted M. Pinaud. Then, just to show that he knew a little about his favourite hobby, he continued:

'They were the first ones to think of putting the radiator at the back of the engine, instead of at the front, as everyone else had done. In those days of flying stones from the road, that was genius.'

'I know. And look at that carburettor — right in the middle and on top of the engine. You can adjust or repair the whole thing without having to touch anything else. On some of these modern cars to-day you have to dismantle half the components before you can even get at the carburettor.'

'And no separate fan with a fan-belt to fray or get slack and snap on a lonely road late at night. Sensible steel fins on the outer casing of the fly-wheel instead. So much simpler, so much more efficient.'

By his last two remarks M. Pinaud could see that he had won the young man's heart. They enthused together for a little longer and then he turned to go.

'Well, I congratulate you, M'sieu —' he looked up at the board above the office door — 'M'sieu Seylan. You certainly have a museum-piece here. Did you buy it from a client?'

'No, m'sieu. As a matter of fact, it was given to me as a birthday present by Madame Laroche.'

'Indeed? I have just left her. I had to go to the *Château* on business.'

'She is fantastically rich. There are rumours in the village that she has about six more vintage cars of this type stored away in her outhouses. I hope to sell this one — that is why I spend all my spare time in polishing it. If you say it is a museum-piece, just imagine what some Arab millionaire will pay for it.'

'Whatever you like to ask, I should think.'

'She has been very good to me. She sent me away to boarding-school — I have no parents — and then to the technical college to learn my trade. And then she financed this garage for me. I wanted to call her *Marraine*, that is godmother, but she would not agree to that. I think there is some kind of family mystery about it all, but she will not tell me what.'

'She is a very determined lady,' M. Pinaud told him with some feeling.

'Yes. But I would do anything for her.'

'Then that is to your credit, M'sieu Seylan. Gratitude is a rare virtue in this world to-day.'

He waited while his tank was filled, paid for the petrol and then moved the car to the other side of the forecourt.

As he got out he noticed that an extension was

being built on to the back of the office. There was a carpenter's bench against the outside wall, beside a large stack of planks and balks of timber, with boxes of tools and kegs of long flat-headed nails left untidily nearby.

He hoped that the young man Seylan was not spending all his profits before he had sold that magnificent vintage car to some Oriental millionaire.

The proprietor of the Eight Bells *café* was a small and genial man, with twinkling and merry eyes and a long and humorous upper lip dominating his elfin and puckish features.

They looked at each other and smiled, and each one liked what he saw.

M. Pinaud spoke first.

'Good-day to you, m'sieu.'

'And to you, m'sieu. What can I do for you?'

'I,' M. Pinaud told him rapidly and firmly — in order to avoid any possible chance of misunderstanding, 'am the possessor of a healthy appetite and a vast and gigantic thirst. The second one is at the moment by far the most important one of the two.'

'And rightly so,' the proprietor agreed gravely, 'since so few people are able to command two such noble possessions at the same time. And what would you like to drink and eat, m'sieu?'

'In this particular region of the country,' M. Pinaud told him quietly and earnestly, 'you will be the first to agree that there must be a noble local wine, completely unknown except to the growers and discerning people like yourself — quite apart from all the celebrated and household names which have justifiably made this locality famous.'

79

'That is quite true,' the proprietor conceded.

'Now I am an old-fashioned type. I do not believe in paying for bottles and fancy labels. I like to pay for what is inside. I am willing to bet that in your cellar here you have some barrels of your local wine. I would be delighted to drink a carafe or two which you could refill without very much difficulty.'

The man looked at him thoughtfully. M. Pinaud felt that he was studying his modest and yet respectable city suit, which he invariably wore when on duty.

'Are you driving, m'sieu?' he asked.

'Yes. I came here by car from Paris.

'Then, if you will excuse me, I must tell you that I am not at all happy at the thought of going down into my cellar and doing what you ask.'

'Why on earth not?'

'Listen, m'sieu – and I will tell you. If you ordered a Pernod, a Campari, a Dubonnet or even a cognac before lunch, I would have no hesitation in serving you. I know what comes out of those bottles when they are poured.

'But this wine of mine – that is something you do not know. But I do. Of this wine one is justified in using the word exceptional. It has a diabolical strength. And since I am talking about something I have known all my life, since I was in the second form at school, you will permit me to observe that I am rather better qualified than you are to know what I am talking about, and therefore it would be a waste of time for you to argue with me.

'If you are driving your car – I presume back to Paris – then I would not recommend our local wine.'

M. Pinaud sat down at the adjoining table, took out his packet of cigarettes and offered one to the proprietor. His voice was grave and serious as he spoke, as befitted the solemnity of the occasion.

'Look, m'sieu – I am the first to appreciate the goodwill that can compel a man to talk a profit out of his own pocket and would like to thank you for your courtesy and concern.

'But let me tell you something you obviously do not know – since I have never seen you before – which is this. That when I drink I drive infinitely better. I have lived with myself and all my faults for a sufficient number of years to know and accept now that this is an undisputed and recognised fact.

'After I have had a carafe – or even two, depending upon the size – of this fearsome local wine you are so reluctant to sell, I will become a part of my car. I will listen to the engine and hear what it is saying. I will pay attention to what the chassis and springs are telling me if I take a corner too fast. I will obey the brakes when they warn me that it is time to put them on.

'This perhaps may sound somewhat fanciful to you, but only because you do not know me. I can assure you that it is the truth.

'All this will help, because I am in a hurry to get back to my wife and children. The more I drink the faster I shall go. Right – now you stop all this nonsense of ruining yourself and go down into that cellar of yours.'

His smile was irresistible, his eloquence compelling. The proprietor's grin threatened to split his face in half.

'Very well, m'sieu. The customer is always right. That is the first rule of innkeeping. Now what about lunch? My wife is the best cook in the *Département*.

81

To-day we have *blanquette de veau*, with peas from the garden.'

'Excellent.'

'Good.'

He turned to go. M. Pinaud stopped him.

'But not now. In about half-an-hour.'

'But —'

'Or even an hour. It may be logical — and even admirable — to hurry in order to get home to one's family, but no-one ever gained anything by hurrying over good food and drink — except perhaps an ulcer. I would like to have reasonable time to verify your opinion of this remarkable local wine.'

'Very well, m'sieu.'

Again he turned to go, and once again M. Pinaud stopped him.

'I shall be delighted to enjoy your wife's cooking, m'sieu, but might I ask her for a bowl of soup first?'

'Of course. Her onion soup is renowned.'

'Good. And perhaps a mushroom omelette to follow, with three or four eggs?'

The grin on the impish face was replaced by a look of dawning respect.

'I did tell you that I had a healthy appetite and that I was hungry,' M. Pinaud felt obliged to add, by way not of excuse but of explanation.

'Certainly, m'sieu. We shall do our best to see that you do not leave these premises until your hunger is satisfied.'

'I have no fears on that account. And if you have a local wine, then obviously you will have a local cheese to finish it all off.'

The proprietor's expression by now was something between awe and reverence. But there was no hesitation in his reply.

'Naturally, m'sieu. And you will be pleased to hear that the local bread came out of the oven about an hour ago.'

Then he finally went down into his cellar.

Some three hours later M. Pinaud was ready for his long drive back home.

The local wine had proved more than worthy of the proprietor's eulogy. He enjoyed and finished two large carafes of it and smoked nearly a whole packet of cigarettes while waiting for his meal.

The wine was incredibly smooth, dry and very slightly astringent, delightfully cool from the atmosphere of the old stone cellar, and possessed a delayed action, he began to think after a while, somewhat comparable to that of a bomb or a land-mine.

He considered that one more carafe was fully justified, if only to do honour to such a magnificent and gargantuan meal, which ended as worthily as it had begun, with a local cheese of unbelievable strength and splendidly delicate creaminess. This tempted him by its very excellence – even though he was only too willing to admit that after two helpings of that fantastic *blanquette de veau* the first edge of his appetite had been very definitely assuaged –to finish half a long French loaf, still warm from the oven.

After a pot of coffee and two glasses of *cognac* he felt satisfyingly replete and at peace with the world.

He paid and thanked the proprietor, complimented his wife on the mastery of her cooking and walked back – perhaps by instinct – the correct way to the garage.

There were three carpenters busily working on the

extension to the office near his car.

One was short and burly, one was tall and thin and the third was a youth with a vacuous and stupid face, bursting out of overalls which fitted him like a sausage-skin. Seylan was still polishing his magnificent car on the far side of the forecourt.

But M. Pinaud was not interested in any of them. He was going home to his beloved wife, and felt — hardly surprisingly — in a mood of exuberant self-confidence which would have encouraged him to bet a week's salary that the journey home was certain to take at least an hour less than the one coming here. If it did, he would be home in time for the exhilarating horseplay of his young daughters' bath.

He got in and started the engine. As a gesture of trust and confidence he had not locked the car.

He backed and turned, and came out on to the main road to Paris. Then he put his foot down hard on the accelerator and tensed himself for some really fast driving.

But he did not drive for long.

He came to a straight stretch of road some kilometres north of the village and flattened the accelerator down to the floorboard.

On either side towered a dense forest, with giant beech-trees growing from the very borders of the road. Ahead it curved very slightly. There was no warning sign denoting a sharp bend. In his mood of delighted exuberance, and excited beyond caution at the thought of getting home in record time, he decided that there was no reason to slow down if he steered expertly into the curve. The surface of the road was good and dry.

There was no-one in the adjacent seat to reason or

84

argue with him. Even if there had been, he could justifiably have refuted any criticism. His decision – even if slightly alcoholic – was perfectly sound and reasonable.

But what he did not and could not anticipate was that in the middle of the curve his two front tyres would suddenly burst and deflate.

Desperately, with all his strength, he fought with the wheel. But the steering was useless. In those precious few seconds his foot had been hard on the brake, but the car was still going fast as it left the curve in the road and smashed into one of the massive trunks of an enormous beech-tree.

His safety-belt and his great strength on the brake saved him from injury.

But the car had been assembled in a hurry on the night-shift in the factory to fleet requirements and the soporific of overtime pay. The tree had stood there, proudly magnificent, for some six hundred years.

There was no doubt as to which one had gained the victory. The front of the car was a mangled wreck. The bark on two of the massive uprising branches was scored and scarred and their wood gouged and splintered and split, but the other three would provide the sap for them to heal.

The front door was jammed. He climbed over the seat, opened the back door and got out, very slowly and shakily, on to the grass verge.

Reaction had set in. All he wanted to do was to lie down and close his eyes. And say a prayer of thankfulness for his miraculous escape. This he did.

Then he forced himself into action. He sprung

open the lid of the boot, grasped the bottom ledge and pulled back with all his strength. The car moved a very short distance and then stopped, jammed and immovable. But this was enough.

Squeezing between the massive uprising branches to one side of the crumped and distorted radiator, the shattered headlights and the mangled wings, he found one long flat-headed nail amidst shreds of torn rubber on what had once been a good round wheel. Any other nails were not apparent, since the second front tyre was no longer visible.

He came around to the back again and walked, very slowly and thoughtfully, from the grass verge to the road, where he waited by the side, facing the direction of Valoisin.

A few moments later an obliging lorry-driver saw him wave and pulled up a short distance in front of him. He lowered the high cab-window and white teeth flashed under a vast and tangled black moustache as he grinned sympathetically.

'These trees have been here for a long time, friend,' he said.

'So I found out – the hard way,' M. Pinaud told him. 'Flat-headed nails in my front tyres. I was fortunate. It could have been much worse. Are you going through Valoisin?'

'Yes. Next place south. Hard luck.'

'Thank you.'

'Any luggage?'

'No. A day trip.'

'Hop in, then.'

'Very kind of you.'

'My pleasure. Hope someone does the same for me one day. Where do you want?'

'The garage, if you please. Seylan is the name.'

'I pass it. I know him.'

'Good. I am hoping he can fix me up with a car to get back to Paris. Have a cigarette?'

'Much obliged to you. There should be no difficulty. After all, it is his trade.'

Seylan the garagist was both concerned and polite.

'Dear me. What bad luck. I thought you left your car rather near those carpenters and their works.'

The burly carpenter, on the other hand, was not only penetratingly loud-mouthed but both truculent and aggressive as well.

'I don't call it bad luck at all, M'sieu Seylan,' he boomed in a voice like a foghorn. 'I call it sheer bloody stupidity — to park a car so near to us and our gear. We are trying to do a job for you in a hurry. A child of twelve could recognise a keg of nails.'

'Lovely — lovely sharp nails,' mouthed the young one, capering about with mindless and apelike excitement. 'I'll get the hammer.'

'All nails have got to be sharp,' put in the tall thin one, making this pronouncement with a sad, profound and most disconcerting melancholy, 'Otherwise how the hell can you drive one into a balk of timber?'

The aggressive one had obviously no time to waste in waiting for an answer to this question.

'Yes, m'sieu,' he bawled out at once. 'You try carrying one of those any distance — and you too might kick a few nails where they should not be. Would you weep if you did?'

'Even if you never got there,' added the young one.

'Which you probably wouldn't.'

'You look a good strong type — but have you any

87

idea what they weigh?'

'Even an idiot knows that a flat-headed nail rolls if one kicks it.'

'And then its own weight brings it up by itself on its head.'

'Then if you are stupid enough to drive a car over it — obviously it goes into the tyre —'

'May I point out,' said M. Pinaud suddenly, loudly and clearly — and interrupting without compunction whatever new and profound contribution to the conversation that the young one was again trying to make, 'that I reversed my car away from your kegs of nails and then turned out of the forecourt.'

'This forecourt,' the burly one roared at him, 'was built to take a pump in the middle of it in order to sell petrol. There it is flat and level, so that honest motorists can get a fair and accurate measure. Everywhere else it slopes. I know. I have had enough trouble with my spirit-level. And I said before that nails will roll if they are dropped and accidentally kicked.'

The young one came forward and clutched his arm.

'Lovely — lovely sharp nails,' he whispered conspiratorially. 'I asked M'Sieu Seylan if he would let me stick some into his customers' tyres while they were getting petrol, so that he could mend the punctures and make more money to —'

'And M'sieu Seylan said no,' interrupted the garagist in a hard, unrecognisable and savage voice. 'That will be enough, Jules. Get on with your work.'

The young one capered off back to the building extension, shouting as he went: 'And then he could give me ten per cent — ten per cent — ten per cent —'

M. Pinaud felt that he was in a mad house. The nail that he had taken from his shredded tyre seemed to be burning a hole in his pocket, but he knew that he would never be able to prove anything.

'I am very sorry indeed about all this, m'sieu,' he heard Seylan saying apologetically. 'If you were a local man you would understand that here we no longer trouble to apologise for Jules. We just accept him and endure him. His parents are thankful that he is not worse — that family has intermarried and reproduced within the prohibited degrees for generations — not only first cousins but brothers and sisters and fathers and daughters as well. It is hardly surprising.

'But I am sure that you, as a reasonable man, will agree that this unfortunate accident can only have been the result of sheer mischance.'

The truculent carpenter waited for M. Pinaud to open his mouth, so that he would be able to shout him down once again. He looked quite crestfallen when M. Pinaud did not speak. He knew that to say anything would be a waste of time. The whole operation had been so diabolically well planned.

He remembered the words Madame Laroche had used. We shall see. She could easily have telephoned Seylan as soon as he had left the *Château*. And he remembered Seylan's own words as well. I would do anything for her.

But there was no proof. Everything this mad trio had stated was completely logical and therefore utterly convincing. He accepted the inevitable and concentrated instead on listening to what Seylan was saying.

'I will send a tow-car to pick up yours at once. And I can easily hire you a car now to get back to Paris. Just a matter of filling in a few forms here in the office. And naturally I shall be pleased to sign any statement on your behalf which will help with your insurance claim.'

'Thank you. That will be a great help.'

He showed his official card and credentials, but from the perfunctory and uninterested glance Seylan gave them he was completely convinced that his identity was already known.

'Would you send your invoice for the repairs to the *Sûreté* at the *Quai d'Orsay*,' he told him. 'I do not carry that sort of money in my pocket-book.'

'Of course, M'sieu Pinaud. I will put it in the post.'

'Thank you.'

'This way to the office. If you would be kind enough to wait a few moments here after you have signed, I will check the hire-car myself and make sure that everything is in order.'

'Thank you once again.'

What else could he say?

He thought how easy it would have been for Madame Laroche, once he had refused her invitation to lunch, to pick up the telephone and ask the proprietor whether he was eating at the Eight Bells, probably the one and only reputable *café* in the village. After all, it was a long drive to Paris. And then to be told that not only was he actually in the *café* but that his car was parked in the garage a few doors away. One more telephone call to a grateful Seylan and the whole thing could have been so easily organised . . .

SEVEN

'Ah yes, Pinaud,' said M. le Chef with not only acid but even venom in his voice, 'I meant to send for you earlier this morning for two reasons, but I have had the Minister himself here all the time without an appointment, which meant the usual lunch. I had to make it now.'

M. Pinaud did not speak. There was no point in saying anything, however inconvenient the summons had been. The great man did what he liked. It would be a waste of time to ask what had prompted such a call from a personage so august and renowned. This must have been business on an extremely high level. Either he would be told or not.

'The first reason is about your car and this second accident. I do not mind telling you that I am beginning to get really annoyed. I told you not to drive so fast. Are you by any chance accident-prone?'

'I do not think so, m'sieu. This was a deliberate attempt to put me out of action.'

'So was the other.'

'Yes, m'sieu. But in either case there is no proof.'

'So you said before. But this is not good enough. That is defeatist talk. There is bound to be proof somewhere. It must be found.'

91

It was all very well for the silly old bastard to talk like that. He would not have to find it. Searching for the needle in a haystack would be child's play in comparison.

'And then the question of expenses for the hire of another one.'

'I had to get back, m'sieu.'

'No-one is arguing about that. But why do you think we maintain an expensive pool of cars here? I could have organised any one of the juniors to fetch you in another one. That would have been far cheaper. They charge for hire by the day, you know.'

'Yes, m'sieu.'

'Yours is not ready yet, I presume?'

'No, m'sieu. That will be a long job.'

'Well then — sign for another one from the pool and get this hired one back at once, or else we shall all be ruined.'

'I will take it back first thing in the morning.'

'Not to-night?'

'No. The garage will almost certainly be closed by the time I get there, and Valoisin is an awkward place from which to catch a train back. The station is no-where near. May I ask you to organise a junior as you suggested to drive a pool car down there with me? I will arrange all the details.'

'Very well. That seems to be the only way to get this hired car back.'

With one of his characteristic lightning-like changes of mood, M. le Chef's voice had suddenly become almost human. So much so that M. Pinaud felt emboldened to say something else.

'May I remind you, m'sieu, that I have hardly seen my family since this case started.'

M. le Chef looked at him thoughtfully for a long time. When he replied there was both kindness and compassion in his voice.

'I have often thought, Pinaud, that a dedicated and successful detective has no business in ever getting himself married. His profession is not fair to his wife nor to his family. But in all fairness to you I will own that each time I have thought about this I have admitted that you are undoubtedly the one exception to the rule. You seem to have made the best of both worlds, in a way that surely must be unique.'

He paused again, for just as long. M. Pinaud waited and did not speak. Praise from one who ate four-hour lunches with a Minister was not declaimed to such a worthy and eminently suitable audience every day. This was an occasion. This was a rarity. This was an event fit to be recounted, with necessary embellishments, to his beloved wife, when and if he ever got home.

M. le Chef continued to look at him during a third and even longer silence, still with that same air of thoughtful consideration. Twice he began to speak, and twice he checked himself. For a man of his character and temperament he seemed strangely ill at ease.

Any other, and lesser man, M. Pinaud reflected as he watched him, might have fidgeted. But a man like M. le Chef did not fidget. And it seemed to M. Pinaud, as they both waited there in that long silence, one sitting and one standing, that there was something in the way that iron self-restraint was imposed which was far more significant than any number of futile gestures would have been.

Twice he opened his own mouth to speak, and

twice a hand, with complete finality, waved imperiously to silence him.

He wondered why.

Then at last M. le Chef decided to begin. In this instance the beginning seemed also the middle and the ending as well. The words now poured out in a torrential flow, quite impossible to interupt, even if one were foolish enough not to know the inviolable rule of the establishment, that no-one ever did presume to interrupt the great man when he was speaking.

'In the past, Pinaud,' he said rapidly, 'you have questioned, criticised, contradicted, impeded, frustrated, annoyed, goaded, hindered, baffled, thwarted and even obstructed me. But you have never let me down. I knew, whatever your sometimes completely unorthodox opinions, that I could always rely utterly and completely on you. I knew that I could always trust you. Implicitly.'

He paused for the first time to take a deep breath. There was only one thing to be said. M. Pinaud said it.

'Thank you, m'sieu.'

'There is no need to thank me. We are dealing with facts. Therefore — in view of what I have just said — in all fairness there is something I must tell you.'

M. Pinaud wondered what it was, but did not speak.

'How are you getting on with these Capets?'

'Not very well, m'sieu. Two of them, the father and the son, are prime suspects, but there is no proof. As I told you, either of them could have killed Laroche and stuck a sharp knife into my tyres the other night. But again there is no proof. And as I mentioned before, I find it hard to believe that either one is a murderer.'

'And as I replied to you on that occasion, Pinaud,

it is the most unlikely person who commits a murder. You ought to be the one to know that, with the vast amount of experience you must have acquired from all your cases.'

'I do, m'sieu. That is why I shall never give up.'

'What will you do if I decide to take you off this case?'

The question was completely unexpected, but there was no hesitation in his reply.

'Go on myself until I have found the murderer.'

'With all that such a decision implies?'

'What exactly do you mean by that, m'sieu?'

'Immediate dismissal. No salary to pay your bills. No insurance. No pension for your old age.'

M'sieu le Chef's voice was expressionless. But again – in spite of the horrifying picture each quiet and emotionless word flashed before M. Pinaud's vivid imagination – there was no hesitation at all in his reply.

'Yes, m'sieu. There are certain principles which hold a man's self-respect.'

There was a long silence. To M. Pinaud it seemed incredibly brief.

The words he had just spoken seemed to flow towards and surge into his mind, over and over again, like the successive waves of an endless and shoreless sea – a sea before him so vast and limitless that he felt small and lonely and afraid. Yet with all the surging and the curling and the breaking of each similar wave the words seemed to bring to him a comfort and a peace which were far greater than his own insignificance, his loneliness and his fear.

They were good words. He felt thankful that he had found enough courage to say them.

Then M. le Chef sighed heavily, took up a sheet of perfectly blank notepaper and studied it intently before he spoke. His words were completely unexpected.

'I quite agree, Pinaud,' he said at last. 'That is why I decided to tell you myself — personally and in this manner. With anyone else there would have been no need. My signature on an official memorandum would have been enough. After all, I am supposed to be in charge here. I am the one who makes the decisions.'

'It would help, m'sieu,' M. Pinaud began patiently, 'if perhaps you told me —'

'That is exactly what I am engaged in doing, Pinaud,' came the swift interruption. There was one short pause before he continued to speak.

'I am under pressure, very strong and influential pressure, to relegate this case to the unsolved file.'

M. Pinaud stared at him in amazement.

'Pressure from —'

'From Madame Laroche and her pet Minister. He is the one who came to see me to-day. This is what it was all about. She is the one who telephoned me at home last night. She wanted to know your home address, which I gave her. Had I refused, she could easily have found out from someone else.

'She is his friend and he is her friend. Although in her case and because of her enormous wealth the relationship has little to do with friendship. It is more a matter of master — or rather, mistress and servant. She gives the orders and he obeys them.'

'But — but this is incredible. Do you mean to say —'

'Of course I do, Pinaud. Or else I would never say it. Not openly, of course — never openly — but all these things, it is well known, can always be arranged or managed.

'You have no idea of the fantastic and frightening power that inherited wealth, in spite of centuries of wars and revolutions, still wields in this country today. Of course, that is not surprising — your own life moves in rather different circles.

'But believe me — and I know what I am talking about — that wealth is still with us and all around us, even greater and infinitely more powerful with the advent and development of civilisation, just as it always has been since murder was committed in the beginning to seize it.

'And in remote parts of the country, such as Valoisin, it had centuries before the efficiency of transport to grow stronger and conceal itself even more effectively and to consolidate. New names, new identities, new records, land-purchase on a vast scale — everything has a price.

'True power, which is wealth, does not die, as kings and emperors, generals and dictators all die in the end. True power does not die. It only goes underground and sleeps — so that it can awake again when the time and the environment are opportune and appropriate.'

He finished speaking and there was silence. M. Pinaud shivered. It seemed that the beautiful room had suddenly grown cold.

That was quite a speech, he thought swiftly to himself. The more so coming from a man who himself was a scion of one of the noblest families in France, who had deliberately turned his back on all the privileges and advantages he had inherited and just enumerated, in order to devote his career and his brilliant intellect to the enforcement of justice.

97

Which meant not to enjoy the manifold pleasures modern civilisation has the power to bring to unlimited wealth — not to enjoy the heady intoxication of an unquestioned power that needed no more effort to implement than the lifting of a telephone receiver — but to spend his life in dealing with torture and murder, degradation and shame, perversion and injustice, robbery, assault and violence. With all their unpleasant and dangerous associations . . .

It was also an interesting pronouncement — all the more because he knew that it was completely true. In spite of the remark that his life moved in different circles, the astonishing experiences and the amazing variety of his numerous cases were sufficient to confirm the veracity of each and all of the statements he had just heard.

Then M. le Chef laid the sheet of notepaper down exactly in the centre of his desk.

'I was glad and thankful — and may I add honestly proud — to hear your decision, Pinaud,' he said quietly. 'I never had the slightest doubt as to what it would be. If I say that it was only what I expected after what I told you, them I am paying you the compliment you deserve.

'Now then, we have worked together long enough to understand each other. It is obvious that my hands are tied. I am bound to accept and obey orders in the same way that you have to. How can I help you?'

'Thank you, m'sieu. At the moment I have no idea where to go or what to do. I have suspicions and theories, but I have no proof.'

'Then the best thing is for you to disappear — what do you think of that?'

'A very good idea.'

'Right. Then I have not seen you since you came in last time. You are still working on this case, according to your first instructions, but you have not told me where you are or what you are doing. Go home to-night and tell your wife the same thing. And tell her to confirm this if she should be questioned. Tell her to say it has often happened in the past and that she does not worry.

'Now you organise a junior to drive a pool car down there with you to-morrow morning, as you suggested. Take him to the station afterwards. Tell him to inform me that you will be in touch. After that you are on your own.'

'Thank you, m'sieu.'

'It is not much, I am afraid. You realise that all I can do is to find you a very little more time – to delay the inevitable for a few days at the most. We are up against a power that is impossible to fight.'

'I understand that, m'sieu. Therefore may I say how very much I appreciate your help.'

'There is no-one who deserves it more than you.'

Then the hard shrewdness of the pale sardonic eyes seemed to melt with the genuine warmth and friendliness of his smile.

'And although I said we only had very little time, there is one thing I would most earnestly like to impress upon you.'

'And what is that, m'sieu?'

'Take care. Don't drive so fast.'

He found an eager young detective named Blanchard, who welcomed enthusiastically the idea of a drive in the country as a happy change from the monotony of studying official forms, gave him the route to Valoisin and arranged where to meet him at eight o'clock the following morning.

The hired car was to be returned to the garage and he would come back to Paris by train, since M. Pinaud had as yet no idea of what he would be doing.

Then he went to the pool and signed for another car.

After all this he went home to his beloved wife and over their late supper told her everything that had happened, as was his habit.

And as always, he minimised the dangers and exaggerated the characters he had met, so that she forgot to worry and to torment herself about the risks of his profession and spent most of her time instead in listening enthralled to the recital of his activities and laughing at his jokes.

Which was, he reflected, as it should be. She had enough worries and anxieties with being a successful mother to two young children without his adding to them.

He began to describe the appearances and the characters of the carpenters at the garage in Valoisin and cunningly showed her a note at the same time on which he had written M. le Chef's instructions as to how to answer any questions during his absence.

In this way he ensured that she saw and understood what was needed without any real comprehension or realisation of the true import of their meaning or even any implication of what the results of these two gentlemen's decision might entail as a consequence, since she was far too busy laughing at the deafening voice of the aggressive one, the disconcerting melancholy of the thin one and the capering antics of the half-witted young one.

Then suddenly the door-bell rang.

Wondering, since he was not expecting any visitors, he went to open the door.

It was the watchmaker Capet.

'Good-evening, M'sieu Pinaud. I hope I am not disturbing you —'

'Not at all. Come in and have a drink.'

'Well — that is very kind of you. My family have spoken very highly of you, M'sieu Pinaud. That is why I have found the courage to come to see you here. But I am afraid I am not a drinking man.'

'That does not matter. I am. I would be far richer in pocket and much better in health if I were not. But I was brought up by a father who could hardly wait until his son was old enough to enjoy a glass of wine with him.

'But on the whole I have no regrets. At least I have found that when things begin to hurt so terribly, as they seem to do more and more these days, such as after thoughtless and hurtful remarks from anyone who is dearly respected or loved, it certainly does dull the sharpness and the torment of the pain to contemplate them through the bottom of a glass.'

He wondered why he should be talking so much. This man, either quite certainly or even very probably, could well be the murderer of Edmond Laroche.

And yet he was a sympathetic type. Ever since he had seen him in his flat with his family, some kind of intuitive reasoning, some instinctive awareness, had convinced him that neither possibility was likely.

But then, he remembered with a vividness that was poignant both in its humility and in its acuity — how many times had he been completely wrong in his assessments of so many murderers in so many cases?

'But here am I – wasting valuable drinking time by talking about it. Come on in and sit down, M'sieu Capet.'

'Thank you.'

Germaine had tactfully disappeared into the kitchen. He waved the watchmaker to a chair in the living-room and produced a bottle of wine and two glasses from the sideboard.

'Thank you once again – just a small one. I understand that you have been down south to Valoisin to see his mother.'

M. Pinaud stared.

'How did you know that?' he asked quietly. 'I told no-one.'

'She telephoned me. She wants me to call to collect a singing bird-box for repair. I came to ask if you would be going there again. It will take me all day to go there and back by train and I simply cannot afford to lose so much time from my work. Your very good health, M'sieu Pinaud.'

'And yours.'

As he drank he thought. He was not supposed to take anyone with him whilst on official business. But to every rule there was always an exception. These were unusual circumstances. This man was not only a prime suspect but also interested him.

Then, with one of those rare flashes of insight into human nature which were to make him famous, he set down his empty glass firmly and asked a question.

'Are you sure there is no other reason why you wish to go with me?'

There was no hesitation in the man's reply.

'Yes, there is. I was glad when she telephoned. I want to see Madame Laroche myself and talk to her

102

about the birth of Yvonne's child. The firstborn of a Capet is and always has been a son. He must have a name. If necessary there will have to be a marriage. She has unlimited power and money. These things with official records and certificates can always be arranged provided the price is right.'

He sipped a second very small mouthful of wine and set the glass down on the polished wood of the table with a delicacy of touch that did not make a sound. M. Pinaud saw that the glass was still half-full and noticed once again the powerful and yet beautiful grace of his hands.

'We do not like bastards in our family,' Capet continued. 'As I told you before, I have my pride.'

M. Pinaud looked at his own glass. It was astonishing how quickly it seemed to be full again.

'Fair enough,' he said. 'Very well. I will take you there, M'sieu Capet, to-morrow morning, if you do not mind getting up early.'

'Not at all. Whenever you like. That is very kind of you.'

'And also if you have no objection to taking the train back, as I do not know yet what I shall be doing myself.'

'Of course. That in itself will be a great help.'

M. Pinaud emptied his glass swiftly. He had found, with the passing of the years, that drinking stimulated his thoughts.

If he took Capet with him in his own car on the following day, he would not be able to talk much or watch any reaction to his questions, as even if it was a long drive it was still a fast one, and on a fast drive the one at the wheel had to watch the road and not the passenger beside him. Should he tell him to get

103

in the hired car with Blanchard to-morrow morning and meet him at Seylan's garage?

He thought about this problem until he noticed that his glass was once again empty. He reached for the bottle and held it out to Capet. But his glass was still at the same level and he waved the bottle away. Almost absent-mindedly, still occupied with his problem, M. Pinaud refilled his own and took a gigantic swallow.

No. Definitely not. This man, in spite of all mitigating appearances and circumstances, might well be a murderer. One did not allow a prime suspect to travel with a junior detective who had not yet mastered the multiplicity of official forms he might soon be called upon to fill in.

One took him in one's own car, and even if preoccupied with driving fast one threw in the occasional apt and apposite remark, and then one listened and maybe — if fate were kind — there might be a clue.

There was always a chance that while he himself was concentrating on driving his passenger might talk. With a little encouragement. This it was his duty to supply. For this he was paid. Inadequately, it was true. But the whole thing was in the nature of a contract. His side of the bargain he was bound to honour, if only for the sake of his own personal pride and his very self-respect.

He looked at his glass. Inexplicably, that one swallow seemed to have succeeded in emptying it. He took the bottle in his hand and poured what was left in it as he spoke.

'On my way home from your flat the other night, M'sieu Capet,' he said quietly, 'I had a nasty accident, and was fortunate in escaping without serious injury. Someone inserted a sharp knife-blade just far enough into my two front tyres so that the air would escape slowly enough not to alarm me and so that they would blow out and burst at speed.'

'Indeed?'

Not a muscle moved in Capet's features. His voice was non-committal, betraying nothing more than a polite interest. His whole attention, one of awed fascination, seemed to be concentrated on M. Pinaud's glass.

'Yes. I found it hard to believe myself. In such a respectable neighbourhood, in which no-one could have either anticipated or expected my visit —'

'It was once a respectable neighbourhood,' Capet interrupted him with a mild and disinterested regret. 'But no longer now. What with all these alien types pouring into the country, seeking and obtaining citizenship, in spite of different morals, standards of living and even religion — things have definitely changed for the worse. It was respectable when we moved there, some fifteen years ago. Now I feel sometimes that I am living in another country.'

So that is your story and you are sticking to it, thought M. Pinaud swiftly. And how can I prove it wrong?

He saw that his glass was empty and moodily went to the sideboard to get out another bottle.

'I can assure you, M'sieu Pinaud,' Capet continued with a convincing and sincere earnestness, 'that I was with my wife and daughter all the time you were interviewing my son, and that he was with them both while you were talking to me.

'We are and always have been a united family. For us, our association with you, in spite of our personal regard for your tact, courtesy and good manners, has been a trial, a burden and a shame.'

All right, thought M. Pinaud swiftly. I am not making much progress with this one. If he is my prime suspect, then it looks as if we have an unsolved murder on our hands.

To-morrow, he decided, he would talk to Capet in the car about his family. Perhaps a clue might be there.

He told his visitor about all the arrangements for the eight-o'clock rendezvous he had made with Blanchard for the morning, and then he escorted him, still expressing his thanks, to the front door and closed it firmly behind him.

Germaine was still in the kitchen. By now she would have finished washing up and laying the table for his early breakfast. This annoyed him mildly, because he always liked to help her with these small but exacting tasks whenever he was at home.

There was still plenty left in the second bottle of wine. Since there was nothing else for him to do, he thought, he might as well go in there and continue his intensive – although completely unproductive – thinking about this character Capet, his prime and only suspect – against whom he had no proof whatsoever.

Germaine would probably be mending stockings in the kitchen. She would not disturb him, knowing that after such an unexpected visit he would be fully occupied.

Then, when he had finished the bottle he could go in to see her. She would make him a pot of scalding hot black coffee. After that and two or three glasses of *cognac* he should be ready for bed.

EIGHT

M. Pinaud had been correct in his assumption that the watchmaker Capet would talk in the car.

But during the first hour, after they had contacted Blanchard in the hired car and crossed the Seine to take the N.7, his words were mainly gabbled prayers for the safety of his body and the absolution of his soul should he die on this road unconfessed and unshriven.

And therefore his talk did little to help towards the solving of this difficult case.

These words were muttered beneath his breath as he sat rigid and tense, hands clenched in torment, terrified at the speed with which M. Pinaud hurled the powerful car through the dense oncoming early-morning traffic.

Blanchard had been given the route and told to follow as best he could. M. Pinaud did not believe in wasting time. The rendezvous would be at Seylan's garage in Valoisin.

But gradually, as the time passed and Capet observed the supreme mastery of M. Pinaud's driving and noted the superb timing and judgment which seemed to dissolve every dangerous situation into mere routine, he began to relax.

His fingers unclenched, the fists became hands and his body sank lower into the comfortable seat. He even fumbled inside his safety-belt and produced a packet of cigarettes which he held up beside the wheel when the road was clear.

'Thank you.'

A light was held to the tip and he puffed out a cloud of smoke with great satisfaction.

'Tell me, M'sieu Pinaud,' said Capet. 'Do you always drive as fast as this?'

M. Pinaud shot the car around an octogenarian who was nursing a small vintage saloon along very carefully at a snail's pace in the middle of the fast lane and laughed as he answered.

'No – no – usually much faster. You ought to be with me when I am alone.'

Capet laughed too. Suddenly between them there seemed to be a palpable easing of tension and strain. Imperceptibly, taking some considerable distance over the operation, M. Pinaud slowed down his speed considerably as he thought exactly what to say.

Now they had left the motorway. Now there were isolated towns with the main road becoming the one high street through them between rows of shops. Now there were lonely villages with green lawns in front of beautiful old houses, now there were massive, isolated and crumbling churches, now there were fields and farms on either side, now there were woods and trees.

He drove on through all of them, thinking and choosing his words before he spoke with the utmost care. This was important. This man was really his one and only suspect. And this man was with him now, because of his own contriving, sitting beside him in the car.

'When I spoke to your daughter Yvonne the other night, M'sieu Capet, I had the impression that she was genuinely in love with this Edmond Laroche. To her, I gather that what he showed her was like a new and different world — something that she had never known before.

'But from the way she spoke to me to tell me about it, and the way she recounted her impressions, I had the feeling that somehow he was sincere, that he was not trying only to impress her with all his money, but showing her all that she could have and enjoy herself, once they were together.'

Capet lowered the window and threw out his cigarette.

'That is what I myself hoped and prayed was happening. What father ever gives up dreaming that his daughter will make a successful marriage? As you know, he met her quite by chance. There was an urgent repair of one of his singing bird-boxes and I sent her there to deliver it.

'With any other man this could have been for her the chance of a lifetime. But when I went to see him he was rude and arrogant. I could not get near him. I could neither talk nor reason with him.

'Having made her pregnant, I thought that at least he would listen to me — her father — and to what I had to say. But to hear him talk anyone would have thought that I was asking him a favour or begging for charity. That is something I could not accept. We Capets have our pride. I was not asking him for any favour. I was only trying to protect my daughter.

'Then he became offensive and insulting, as I have told you.'

'What do you intend to do now — when you get there?'

'I maintain that Madame Laroche, as his mother, owes me something — according to my own personal thinking. He was her son. He is dead. She is his mother. She is alive. She has both money and power. I feel that my debt is a just one. That is why I am sitting here beside you now, on my way to collect it.'

For a long moment there was silence. Then M. Pinaud, driving with one hand and a familiarity born of long practice, extracted his own packet of cigarettes from his pocket and offered it to Capet.

'I do not think you have the slightest hope of succeeding,' he said quietly. 'That woman is too hard and too merciless.'

'Thank you.'

Capet held up his lighter.

'You may be right. I do not know. But I do know that it is upon me to try, for the sake of my family honour and my own pride and self-respect.'

M. Pinaud was silent as he increased his speed considerably for the next few kilometres. Part of his mind was concentrating on the problems of the traffic on the road, the other part was wondering what else this man might have been driven to do for the sake of those same principles which were obviously so dear, so important and even so sacred to him.

His wondering achieved nothing, except the blare of infuriated horns from exasperated motorists when the two parts of his mind happened momentarily to merge . . .

How could he arrest a man on suspicion of murder because of his ideological beliefs? How could he arrest and charge a man without proof? And that was the

110

one thing he did not have.

And so, in due course, without anything more important being said, they came to Valoisin and Seylan's garage.

Thanks to M. Pinaud's driving, Blanchard was still a great distance behind on the N.7 when they pulled up in the forecourt.

The carpenters were no longer there, M. Pinaud noticed. The extension to the office was still unfinished. Perhaps, he thought swiftly and sardonically – and not without a certain bitterness – they were only summoned to work on occasions when interfering detectives had to be summarily dealt with . . .

Seylan came out of his office, smiling and bland.

'Ah – good-morning. It is M'sieu Pinaud from Paris – yes?'

Seylan's cheerful voice successfully interrupted this morose and unprofitable train of thought. He therefore dismissed it quickly.

'Yes. Good-morning to you. A certain M'sieu Blanchard will be here shortly to return your hired car. Would you be kind enough to deal with all the necessary papers and accept his signature on my authority, to tell him that we are going on now to the *Château* and to ask him if he would wait here for me until I come back.'

'Certainly, m'sieu.'

'Thank you very much.'

One half of the immense nail-studded front door of the *Château* opened noiselessly on well-oiled hinges and Charles, the same dignified manservant, now clad in a different and yet even more beautifully cut suit, eyed them with lofty condescension.

111

'Good-morning, gentlemen. May I help you?'

'Good-morning to you,' M. Pinaud replied with equal politeness. 'You no doubt remember me. The name is Pinaud, from the *Sûreté*. This gentleman is M'sieu Capet. We would both like to see Madame Laroche for a few moments.'

Charles glanced from one to the other. M. Pinaud could have sworn that there was pity behind the condescension. Nevertheless, he held the half-door open wider as he spoke.

'Would you please come inside, gentlemen. I regret to say that visitors are never received here in this house without a prior appointment. But naturally — since you are here — I will inform Madame immediately of your arrival.'

They entered the enormous hall.

'Please to be seated, gentlemen. I will not keep you waiting long.'

He was as good as his word. They had hardly sat down and made themselves comfortable when he reappeared.

'I have been instructed to inform you, gentlemen,' he announced pontifically, 'that Madame is at the moment engaged with Mademoiselle de Granson in a very important conference concerning the business affairs of the shop in the Rue de La Paix.'

He paused and drew in a deep breath, obviously meticulously co-ordinating mentally his last specific instructions, in case he should commit an unpardonable sin of getting them in any way confused. Then he continued to speak.

'Madame does not wish and has not the slightest inclination to see M'sieu Pinaud again. She will be pleased to receive M'sieu Capet in half-an-hour's

112

time, when the conference should be over. She told me to ask you, M'sieu Capet, whether you would prefer to wait here or call back. The decision is entirely yours.'

M. Pinaud was hardly surprised at her refusal to see him. At the moment he accepted it. This was not the time to insist. He still had no proof.

Then he looked at Capet.

'Which do you prefer?' he asked.

'I will wait here, if you do not mind. I have nowhere else to go. I will take the train back.'

'Very well. I will return to the garage.'

He got out of the comfortable chair and stood up.

Charles looked at him once and then spoke to Capet. In that brief glance, behind the pity and the condescension, he could now definitely read contempt. A man whom Madame did not wish to see was obviously not worth any attention at all. But to Capet he was cordiality and civility personified.

'I will bring you refreshment, M'sieu Capet, the morning newspapers and magazines. The tradition of hospitality in this house has remained unchanged ever since it was a monastery and the Abbot himself came down to wash the feet of pilgrims and mendicants before he fed and clothed them.'

He opened the half-door courteously for M. Pinaud and yet managed to convey in that one efficient and all-embracing movement how delighted he was that Madame had managed to deal so successfully with such riff-raff as unsolicited callers.

Very thoughtfully M. Pinaud went back to his car.

He was not worried so much about his feet. He took a bath quite often. But as he made a point of wearing his one and only best suit — now definitely beginning to show the first signs of wear — whenever he was on duty and engaged in a case, it would have been nice, he thought, had he lived some nine hundred years ago when the Abbot himself might well have re-clothed him.

And given him refreshment. Already, after that long fast drive, the first stirrings of his gargantuan appetite reminded him that he was hungry. And he also had a thirst. A noble thirst.

He sighed profoundly. It was a pity that he had not been born nine hundred years before.

The road back to the village from the end of the *Château* drive was narrow and winding, between high hedgerows and through rich and undulating farm land.

He saw a large and prosperous looking farmhouse ahead on his left, dominating the rising and rolling fields, protected and sheltered by belts of huge and ancient trees. The sheds and outbuildings for the animals were on the far side with gaps in the hedgerows and entrances to the road on either side.

He was preoccupied with all his thoughts and yet he drove with his usual care and concentration, noticing subconsciously that around these entrances the road surface was covered with mud and droppings from tractors with their overloaded trailers.

He saw a heavy lorry come out of one of the farm lanes on his left, turn and approach him. There was just enough room for the two vehicles and therefore he did not reduce his speed.

The lorry was accelerating from its turn out into the road. They approached each other in a sea of mud, slime and cattle-droppings from the two entrances to the fields on either side.

114

Just before their radiators crossed the lorry driver jammed on his brakes, locked his wheels and in a beautifully controlled skid smashed into his car and flung it off the road into the nearby ditch.

The whole operation seemed instantaneous and therefore all the more terrifying. M. Pinaud's windscreen was starred and opaque with the shock. Quickly he released his safety-belt. Then he tried the front door, but the heavy iron girders in the lorry's frame had jammed the lock. He then climbed over the seat. The back door was free.

He got out, not without some difficulty and several deep scratches from the massive hedge about the ditch, came to the entrance and the road.

The lorry had pulled up very quickly in a comparatively short distance. Its side did not seem to have a scratch. The driver had been running back towards the car, but when he saw M. Pinaud he slowed to a walk.

Then M. Pinaud saw the second ghost of the man who had lain, sightless and unseeing, on a tray in the morgue in Paris. Seylan had been one. This one was the other. The one had been fair. This one was dark. They could have been twin brothers.

'I say,' he called out in a loud voice well before they were together, 'I really am most frightfully sorry. Are you all right? Are you hurt?'

M. Pinaud answered automatically. His mind was filled with furiously racing thoughts.

If ever he had seen or heard of a deliberately provoked accident, this was it. From the rising land around the farm, his approach could have been noted by anyone sitting and waiting in the driving seat of a lorry, especially if alerted beforehand by a telephone-call from the *Château* as to what time he had left.

There was only one road to the village. He had told both Seylan and Capet, in the presence of the manservant Charles, that he was taking it to go back. And to an experienced driver, a controlled skid was child's play. A truck-load of mud and slime could have been prepared beforehand, on receipt of a first telephone-call from Seylan, as soon as they had left his garage. And then, with a tractor, tipped out and shovelled to prepare the road in time for the accident, as soon as they had passed the entrance to the field.

'I am all right, thank you,' he replied quietly. 'A little shaken, I do not mind admitting. I was fortunate to escape. But I am afraid my car is a wreck. It has not got the weight of your lorry.'

'No need to worry about that,' the man replied cheerfully. 'My insurance will gladly pay, whatever the cost. I freely admit – contrary to their specific instructions – that all this was entirely my own fault.'

M. Pinaud took out a cigarette. He noticed that his hand was trembling as he held the flame of his lighter to its end. He did not offer the packet to the other man.

'What I fail to understand, M'sieu –'

'My name is Cardin.'

'M'sieu Cardin – what I find somewhat difficult to understand and appreciate – when we were both passing each other on a road wide enough for two – is why you should suddenly jam on your brakes and naturally enough, on a road surface such as this, skid into my car.'

Cardin was completely unabashed, supremely confident and entirely self-assured.

116

'I told you already. It was entirely my own fault. I have a load of wood-logs in the back. Just as we were coming together, I suddenly remembered what the road surface was like outside this field and thought that perhaps I might get into a slide.

'My tyres are by no means new and although perhaps as a townsman you do not know, unseasoned wood holding water can be a very tricky load. I had been accelerating after coming out of the farm and so I jammed on my brakes. Then I got in a skid and out of control.'

M. Pinaud inhaled deeply on his cigarette.

'So that is your story,' he said slowly and thoughtfully. And also very distinctly. The careful wording of his phrase was deliberate, purposely provoking.

For a second there was a flash of hostility in the dark eyes. For a second the evil that had been Edmond Laroche his father spread like a stain with the surge of blood across his features.

'Yes, that is my story. I have no intention of changing it, M'sieu — I also do not know your name —'

'My name is Pinaud, from the *Sûreté*. And I would bet money, M'sieu Cardin, that you already know my name.'

'You would lose your bet, M'sieu Pinaud. I have already told you that I am willing to admit full and unquestioned liability for this unfortunate accident, which was entirely my own fault. If you wish to pursue the matter further and sue me legally, I can assure you that you would be wasting your time. There are no witnesses. You and I are alone. It is your word against mine. I have already admitted the fault. No lawyer in his right senses would ever advise you to go to court.'

117

'No. Maybe you are right.'

'I know I am right. Can I at least offer you a lift to the village? I gather you were going there?'

'I was.'

M. Pinaud threw away his cigarette and looked at him directly.

'But now I have changed my mind. I am going back to the *Château*.'

He noted with satisfaction a flash of what could have been concern or even dismay in the dark eyes regarding him so intently.

'But —'

'I shall be pleased to accept your kind offer, M'sieu Cardin. As you were obviously going in that direction, it should not be too much trouble.'

'Of course not. As you wish. Jump in, then.'

His tone was indifferent. M. Pinaud climbed up into the high front of the cab, took out his packet of cigarettes, lit one and again did not offer the packet.

Cardin started the engine and drove off towards the *Château*. With one hand he took out his own packet of cigarettes and lit one. Neither man spoke.

As they reached the end of the short journey and the entrance to the drive, M. Pinaud uttered five short words.

'Thank you. This will do.'

'What about getting back?' Cardin asked, his engine still running. 'There are cars here and someone could drive you.'

'No, thank you. I prefer to walk.'

'As you wish.'

For a moment they stared at each other in silence, the hostility and the hate and all the unspoken and unnecessary words seeming to vibrate between them

118

with an almost physical intensity.

Then M. Pinaud opened the door and got out. As he stood on the far side, a large and expensive car swung out of the drive, turned and took the road back to the village. Louise de Granson was driving. She was alone. If she saw him she gave no sign of recognition.

The lorry drove on its way.

There was neither reproof nor condemnation on the manservant's placid countenance, for that would have been a betrayal of the reverend Abbot's traditional hospitality, yet M. Pinaud had no difficulty in recognising the disapproval that lurked rampant in the very depths of those otherwise expressionless eyes.

He made no attempt to open the half-door any wider.

'Madame Laroche is now engaged with M'sieu Capet from —'

'I would know that even if I were an idiot,' M. Pinaud interrupted him hardly and rudely, 'considering that I brought him here myself.'

He was not normally a rude man. Good manners, in his opinion, were essential to good and gracious living. But by now some of the inevitable reaction from the shock of his accident had begun to set in and his nerves were on edge.

'And I do not care if she is. M'sieu Capet can wait. I am going to see Madame Laroche at once. Now. Immediately.'

The disapproval, rapidly and obviously, became sheer consternation.

'But this is unheard of. I would not dare to interrupt or —'

'I would.'

He moved with unbelievable rapidity. His gun was out of its shoulder holster in a matter of seconds and the barrel gently touched the front of that beautiful suit without disturbing in the slightest way any fold of its impeccably rich cloth.

'Enough of this nonsense. Take me to her at once.'

The man stepped back, pulling the door wide-open as he did so, turned and without a word led the way through the endless corridors to that same lovely room M. Pinaud remembered so well.

He knocked on the door and the familiar imperious voice told him to enter.

'Madame – please forgive me – this person has threatened me with a gun –'

M. Pinaud shouldered him aside and stepped into the room. She was sitting in the same chair with Capet opposite in the one that he had occupied before. Both looked at him in astonishment. Madame Laroche kept her eyes on his face. Capet looked down at the gun.

'M'sieu Capet,' he said quietly and courteously, 'would you be kind enough to wait in the entrance hall for a short while. I am sorry to intrude like this on you and your private affairs, but I have official business with Madame.'

Capet stood up at once.

'Of course I –'

The arrogant and imperious voice interrupted him like the hard cut of a knife.

'There is only one person who gives orders in this house, M'sieu Capet, and that –'

'Thank you, M'sieu Capet, for your courtesy.'

And now M. Pinaud's voice was no longer quiet.

120

His interruption had been deliberately as hard and as sharp as her own.

She stared at him in incredulous disbelief. He ignored her and spoke to the manservant.

'Would you kindly take M'sieu Capet with you. And close the door behind you.'

The gun was still in his hand. Capet walked towards him. Charles looked helplessly at Madame Laroche, but she did not say anything. The two men left the room and the door closed.

M. Pinaud replaced his gun and then, reaching into his hip-pocket, took out his handcuffs as he had done beore.

'Madame Laroche,' he said coldly, 'I had these out the last time I saw you and now I have them out again. And I will have no compunction in using them to take you in custody to Paris.'

'You must be mad,' she replied swiftly. Then the words seemed to pour out in a torrent of rage. 'You ought to have your head examined. You have no official status here. You have no power and no authority. No longer. Have you seen your Chief?'

'No. I have not been back since I saw you last. And I have no idea what you are talking about.'

He lied cheerfully and with neither remorse nor hesitation. At least he owed this to the old man who had backed him up, treated him so fairly and helped him in a way that might well have meant the end of his own career.

'Then for you own information, M'sieu Pinaud, I will tell you that you are no longer working on the case of Edmond Laroche. There is no case. It has been closed. You will be given your orders the next time you see or speak to your superiors.'

She paused and drew in a deep breath.

'This forcible entry into my house is an intrusion, and I will see that you are prosecuted and punished. We do not care for interference in our affairs at Valoisin. I am ordering you to leave this house at once.'

He shook his head and swung the handcuffs gently against his thigh.

'No, Madame. I meant every word I said.'

Her eyes darkened with rage.

'You would not dare —'

'Yes, I would. In spite of all your Minister friends and your influence and corruption in high places. This, mercifully and happily, has not reached me yet.'

He had some very good idea of what he was doing, especially after M. le Chef's words — of how he might well be throwing away his whole career and his future, and in consequence depriving his wife and his family and causing them to know poverty and distress. But in him, characteristically, there was never any hesitation. He was only doing his duty as he saw it.

She looked at him for a long moment, during which her rage gradually and yet obviously melted and was replaced by something very like respect, even admiration. This was the first and only time anyone had ever defied her authority.

He had no idea himself of the dignity and majesty of his bearing. To him there could be no question of doubt or compromise. He was only trying to do his work honestly in accordance with his principles, in order to earn a living for his wife and children.

But he could and did notice once again that amazing self-command and co-ordination of mind with which she could adapt herself immediately to any unforeseen situation, and therefore was hardly surprised when her next words, at the termination of that long and appraising silence, were spoken in a reasonable tone and not in a voice literally quivering with uncontrolled rage.

'Why are you here, M'sieu Pinaud — why have you come back to Valoisin? Do you suspect anyone here of the murder?'

'I suspect everyone, Madame,' he replied quietly, and in his voice he too now modulated that hard arrogance with which he had spoken to her formerly. 'That is my profession. I suspect you yourself of thwarting and obstructing justice for the sake of your good name and reputation. I suspect the two illegitimate sons of Edmond Laroche of both trying to injure or even murder me on your instructions, so that I could not continue with an investigation you find an embarrassment. And I suspect your servant Charles as an accomplice for telephoning to give the time that I left here this morning.'

'I do not understand what you mean.'

'Very well. I am sure you do. But I will explain. When I left this house, the last time I saw you, I drove back to Seylan's garage. Flat-headed nails had been inserted into my front tyres so that I had blow-outs and a smash.

'When I brought M'sieu Capet here this morning I told him that I was going back to the garage. This was overheard. There is only one road. A lorry driven by the son who calls himself Cardin skidded deliberately on the mud outside one of his farm entrances and smashed my car into a ditch. How easy for your servant Charles to pick up a telephone and give a little information about my departure in good time.

'At the present moment the charge would only be one of malicious assault, but I could easily have burnt to death and that would have made it attempted or successful murder.'

Her voice did not change. It was polite, reasonable and courteous.

'But both of these were only accidents.'

'Yes. But such fortuitous accidents can so easily and so often be arranged.'

'You have no proof, M'sieu Pinaud.'

Still her voice had not changed.

'Agreed.'

'Then let me tell you something. Both of Edmond's illegitimate sons hated him. Which is hardly surprising. There are always well-meaning and well-intentioned people in a village like this who are only too ready and willing to describe in detail to these two young and intelligent men how their schoolgirl mothers suffered agonies before they died.

'To say they both hated him would be the understatement of the year. I have had an almost impossible task – and an expensive one, I can assure you – to keep them away from him since they were boys and left school.'

'Then either of them, or both, could have taken the train or motored to Paris and called that evening at the Rue de La Paix?'

'Obviously. But then again, M'sieu Pinaud, you have no proof.'

He looked at her steadily and his common sense compelled him to acknowledge and admit that she was right. He had no proof. And what was more, it looked as though he would never have any proof.

'But here in Valoisin,' the calm quiet voice went on,

'here in this part of the world we command loyalty.'

And underneath the calmness and the quietness he seemed to hear the throbbing of a great pride – the pride of tradition, the pride of the centuries-old hospitality of a monastery, a pride in the power and the wealth of her name and her family.

Her features, arrogant and compelling, seemed to emphasise and underline every word she said.

'You talk glibly about taking a train or driving to Paris,' the calm quiet voice continued. 'Both of them could produce a dozen witnesses to swear that they never left this village on the night or the day that Edmond was killed. And my servant Charles will go to court if necessary and swear that neither he nor I used the telephone at all to-day after you left this house. There is a switchboard in the hall. He connects any extension to an outside line. He would make a reliable and trustworthy witness.'

He did not say anything. After a pause she spoke again. There was no triumph in the calm quiet voice, only a placid and logical enumeration of facts.

Where is your case, M'sieu Pinaud? Where is your proof? Suspicions are nothing. You must have proof before you can act.'

Abruptly she stood up. The interview, which she had never granted, was clearly over.

'I would suggest that you go back to Paris yourself, M'sieu Pinaud, and see your Chief. Perhaps what he will have to tell you may put an end, once and for all, to this persecution which is beginning to annoy me.'

In her words, arrogant and self-assured, he caught more than a glimpse of her frightening powers. In her mind it was obvious that there was not the slightest doubt as to the outcome of her request. She had wanted something done and had therefore brought pressure on the man capable of doing it. It would be done. It was already done.

He realised that he could do nothing.

In spite of all his talents – and who knew them better than he did himself? – his intuition and his intelligence, his perseverance and his capacity for hard work, his acumen, his persistence, his logically deductive powers, his insight into human nature, his decisive and conclusive methods of evaluating evidence – in spite of all these outstanding qualities which had finally brought him fame on both sides of the Atlantic – in spite of them all he was powerless.

Whatever this woman had said was true. According to her, he had no proof. And therefore he had no case. She could summon witnesses who would perjure themselves gladly on her behalf. He could summon no-one to uphold his contentions, his deductions or his conclusions.

Whatever he might have had now no longer existed. And he remembered with a pride not unmingled with bitterness that several of his more successful cases had started off with even more difficulty and obscurity.

Now, to add insult to injury, he had been removed. He, the greatest detective of all, had been recalled and dismissed before the case was even solved. He could have wept at the shame and the ignominy of it all.

Fortunately, he remembered in time that famous detectives do not habitually weep in the presence of ladies – not even if they happen to be both rich and powerful – whatever the agonising bitterness of their emotions.

And so, castigating himself mercilessly for even harbouring such a thought, he controlled himself forcefully, said good-morning politely, slipped the handcuffs back into his pocket and left the room.

NINE

It took him forty minutes to get back to the garage. He did not feel very well, and he did not walk very fast.

Reaction had set in, and the nervous tension engendered by his interview with Madame Laroche had given him a gigantic thirst.

'What on earth is the matter with you?' young Blanchard greeted him cheerfully. 'You look like death warmed up. And you have scratches and dried blood all over your face. And I have been waiting here in this forsaken dump for hours.'

'I am sorry about that,' he apologised immediately and contritely. 'I had an argument with a lorry and the lorry won.'

'That will please the boss.'

'I do not dare to think about him. But there is no need to stay any longer – have you signed all the papers for the hired car?'

'Yes. All settled.'

'Good. Then there is no need to wait now. You had better make your way back as soon as you can. I will follow on later. I still have some important business to do here.'

There was no need to tell Blanchard that the

important business, apart from organising Seylan on his wrecked car, was to attend immediately to his clamouring appetite and immense thirst, in case such extraneous facts should inadvertently appear on one of those verbose reports that young man delighted in typing.

'Right. See you later. Look after those scratches — they look nasty to me. What was it?'

'Blackthorn, I should think.'

'Ask the chap here for some iodine or antiseptic. Blood-poisoning won't help you in the middle of a case.'

'Thank you. I will.'

'See you.'

'Bye.'

M. Pinaud watched him go with affection and pity. Affection because of that genuine and sincere concern about his scratches, and pity because he could not possibly know that his respected and revered senior, the shining example to all the juniors in the organisation, was no longer in the middle of a case, but had been summarily removed from any further participation in it . . .

Then he went to see Seylan in his office.

'You will be delighted to hear, M'sieu Seylan,' he announced cheerfully, 'that I have got even more repair business for you.'

Why should he not feel cheerful, he asked himself. He had just had another narrow escape from death or serious injury, and he was the possessor of a gigantic thirst and an enormous appetite, about both of which he was in the fortunate position of being able to do something in the very near future. He remembered the name of the inn, The Eight Bells, with affection, gratitude and anticipation.

Seylan's expression was wary and non-committal, his voice without expression.

'Indeed?'

M. Pinaud thought swiftly that neither he, nor the manservant Charles, nor Madame Laroche herself, had made any comment on his appearance. Only Blanchard. As if scratches and dried blood were naturally to be expected on a man who had just had an accident. About which everyone concerned would have been informed.

'Yes. My car is in a ditch near a farm entrance on the road from the *Château* to here. Would you be kind enough to organise a tow and send us an estimate for repair?'

'How unfortunate. That would be the farm of M'sieu Cardin.'

'Yes. You are quite right. That was the name. His lorry skidded on a patch of mud and crashed right into me. He admitted full liability and so I shall ask our insurance company to get in touch with you both.'

'Very well, m'sieu. Will you be requiring another hired car?'

M. Pinaud looked at him very thoughtfully.

'No, thank you. I do not think so. Shall we say my plans are still a little uncertain?'

'As you wish.'

Seylan seemed completely indifferent. But by now M. Pinaud had come to the conclusion that the fewer people in this village of Valoisin who knew what he was going to do in the near future the better for him — in that the fewer number of telephone calls would be made regarding his movements and his destination.

'Thank you. Good-bye.'

130

The proprietor of The Eight Bells, looking more gnome-like than ever, greeted him with enthusiasm and a happy smile of recognition.

'Why — it is the gentleman who ate the *blanquette de veau* the other day —'

'That is quite right,' M. Pinaud interrupted him cheerfully. 'And drank several carafes of that wonderful wine you were so reluctant to sell me. I do hope you have some left.'

'Of course I have. Please take a table. I will fetch one at once.'

M. Pinaud lit a cigarette and knew that he was going to unwind successfully. When the proprietor returned with a carafe he looked up and smiled.

Please be good enough to get yourself another glass, M'sieu. This wine is too good to drink alone.'

'That is very kind of you.'

The glass appeared in a matter of seconds and the wine was poured with due solemnity.

'Your very good health.'

'And yours, M'sieu. And thank you.'

'And what is Madame your excellent wife cooking to-day?' M. Pinaud asked him, refilling their glasses swiftly. 'I can still taste that incredible veal. If ever she would like me to sign a paper of commendation I am entirely at your service.'

The proprietor eyed him with a great approval over the rim of his glass. This was a man after his own heart.

'She will be delighted when I tell her,' he said. 'Most people take it all for granted. So few trouble to express their appreciation. As a matter of fact, you happen to have come on a good day. *Coq au vin* —

her speciality. With cauliflower cooked to tenderness and then fried in batter.'

M. Pinaud held up his hand.

'Sold. In about an hour's time. And the omelette – and the cheese – that cheese which melted in the mouth –'

The proprietor emptied his glass and stood up with alacrity, purpose and determination.

'I will organise the whole thing at once,' he declared.

M. Pinaud held up his hand.

'Before you go – I am sure that both you and your good wife will understand this – but as I had to get up this morning at the crack of dawn to drive down here from Paris my appetite is considerably greater even than it was the other day. Do you think perhaps that another couple of eggs in the omelette –'

He allowed his voice to die, courteously and doubtfully, on the question. Now it was the proprietor's turn to raise his hand.

'Say no more, m'sieu. Good food needs appreciation. And obviously – since the dish is the whole chicken – you would not wish her to pick out a small one, would you?'

Without waiting for an answer to his question he disappeared behind the bar.

M. Pinaud smiled happily as he refilled their glasses. This was a good and understanding type. He fully deserved to have such a cook for a wife.

The glasses were large. He noticed that the level in the carafe was looking somewhat low. He would have to order another one when the man returned. He seemed to be taking some considerable time in that kitchen over the ordering of what seemed to be quite a simple lunch.

Perhaps he was having trouble with that paragon amongst cooks. Even the best and most estimable of wives, he reflected philosophically — with the wisdom and experience born of many years of marriage — had their off days . . .

He lifted his glass and sipped that glorious wine appreciatively, allowing its cool and astringent taste to transform and exhilarate his whole palate. There was no point in holding up a session of such serious and laudable drinking just because the man chose to stay away so long in his kitchen. He would order another carafe as soon as he came back.

While he was waiting he might as well finish this one.

It could be that she was tired and did not feel well, and the kitchen might be hot and oppressive with the cooking, and therefore it was reasonable to assume that the advent of a husband, who was supposed to be doing his job in looking after customers in the bar, reeking of strong wine and demanding that she change the chicken she had already spent hours in preparing for lunch for a very much larger one in order to please a highly valued and important client — it was quite feasible to assume that such an intrusion in these circumstances might well be received with a marked lack of enthusiasm . . .

But all that had nothing to do with him. He was a client. He was a customer. The problem, if there were one, concerned only the domestic economy of the establishment and its participants.

He had quite enough to occupy his own mind.

What ought he to do now? Where should he go next?

There was no point in going back to the office,

even if he could have accomplished the journey in another wrecked car. M. le Chef had backed him up. He had given him a few more days of precious delay. No-one knew where M. Pinaud was, the word would go out. Somewhere in the process of investigating this difficult case, according to his most recent instructions. Therefore, provided he did not call in to report, he could not be removed to implement any newer and conflicting orders from higher authority.

Besides, quite apart from the considerations of logic and common sense, it would hardly be an act of common courtesy to repay such understanding and help by confronting M. le Chef with a situation which was bound to have its inevitable and injurious effect on his blood-pressure.

He took another large drink and refilled his glass, if only to fortify himself against the hideous scene his vivid imagination so easily and swiftly conjured up before him.

He could hear every word of those acid and sarcastic tones, as clearly as if they were cutting like sharp and vindictive knives through the thin wooden panels that lined the walls of that silent and deserted inn.

'You must be mad, Pinaud — stark raving mad. I told you to drive slowly. You must have heard me telling you to drive slowly. I told you plainly. You are not deaf. Why not listen to me for a change then, and do as I tell you?

'Have you ever paused to consider that perhaps the minds of other people — apart from your own — might also be endowed with intelligence, common sense, logic and reason?

'These crashes are seldom serious if one drives slowly and with due care. One I am prepared to accept, as a reasonable risk in a dangerous profession. Two I would deplore, and verify all the circumstances with the most meticulous and scrupulous care. But not three. Three is too much.

'You can't go about much longer like this smashing up cars wholesale like a lunatic. Every car you sign for you manage to wreck. You will ruin the establishment. Quite apart from killing yourself as well.

'Take my word, there are no flies on insurance companies. They pay once with a pleasant toothpaste smile, but they do not care so much about paying again. Things like bonuses and no-claim discounts have a habit of disappearing and premiums tend to rise for no accountable reasons but innumerable explanations. What do you think will happen when I ask them to pay astronomical repair bills three times in the space of a few days?

'I happen to be running a fleet of cars in this establishment, Pinaud. Imagine what my expenses will be next year if I let you go on like this.

'Have you ever paused to think – while you are holding the wheel and trying to stamp the accelerator through the floor – that I have enough trouble already here because of that mad woman with her medieval mind and her tame Minister giving me orders and telling me how to do my job?'

Now this last question, M. Pinaud conceded fairly, eyeing the empty carafe with a regretful moodiness, was not an easy one to answer. Its irrefutable logic defied not only excuse, but even explanation and argument.

And yet, he maintained with some justification, who would dare to say that any of these accidents had been his own fault?

The appearance of the proprietor from behind the bar put an end to his introspection. There were beads of perspiration both on his brow and upper lip.

'Everything is in order, m'sieu,' he announced, breathing heavily and triumphantly. 'I am sorry to have been so long.'

'Not at all,' M. Pinaud assured him mildly. 'I enjoyed every moment, drinking your delicious wine. I am afraid I could not wait. Your glass is still there. Please finish it and then be kind enough to bring another carafe.'

The proprietor snatched up his glass and drained its contents in one gigantic swallow. Then he took out a vast handkerchief that resembled a tea-towel in its dimensions from his pocket and wiped his face energetically.

Finally he shrugged his shoulders in a most expressive gesture, took up the carafe, ejaculated the one word 'women' with a great and pent-up emotion and walked off towards the cellar.

When he returned, in an incredibly short time, the carafe he set down on the table was approximately twice the size of the one he had taken away.

M. Pinaud stared at it in amazement, opened his mouth to speak and then closed it again. A cheerful and happy smile transformed his features.

Married men, he reflected philosophically, usually found very little difficulty in understanding each other . . .

TEN

Some three hours later M. Pinaud sat back in his chair with a sigh of utter and complete satisfaction.

It had been a memorable meal – the omelette light as a feather, the salad sharp and crisp and nutty, the gigantic chicken melting from off its bones into his mouth and the cheese an aroma almost without substance.

He watched the proprietor bringing in a tray with coffee. On it stood a very old square bottle of colourless glass filled with some pale green liqueur.

'What would that be?' he asked politely.

'That, m'sieu,' the reply came swiftly and without hesitation, 'is a small token of my appreciation – not only for your custom as a client, but also for the courtesy and the generosity with which you have given it.'

Now that, thought M. Pinaud, was a speech many politicians with great power in the government might do well to study as a model of decorum and tact.

'Thank you,' he said quietly.

'This is a liqueur,' the proprietor continued, 'distilled from plums by the same family of farmers who have supplied our wine for seven generations. I do not need to say any more. Whatever has to be said will be said by you after you have tasted the first glass.'

He poured two cups of scalding hot coffee and then solemnly filled two large wine-glasses to the brim with the pale green liqueur.

'Your very good health, M'sieu Pinaud,' he said quietly, raising one to his lips.

M. Pinaud looked at him with astonishment. But immediately he drank as well.

'And yours, m'sieu. You know my name?'

'Of course. Everyone in this village knows your name. I feel that I should tell you this. It is a small village. Everyone talks and everyone knows what is going on. I have heard enough.'

M. Pinaud thought swiftly and rapidly. An excess of alcohol might well have the disastrous effects which his beloved wife always grasped as a reason and a justification for so righteously reprimanding him on any justifiable occasion when – under its influence – he might have transgressed, but there was no doubt at all that it stimulated his creative thinking when he was in the middle of a case.

'In view of what you have just told me, m'sieu –' he began quietly and carefully. Then he paused. He was compelled to pause.

The enormous mouthful of the liqueur he had just swallowed seemed to reach up again, from the lower depths of his stomach, to spread and unfold, heated and expanded by the mouthful of scalding hot coffee he had also imbibed on top of it, spreading out and expanding as if the very plums themselves were boiling and bubbling and generating their own exquisite aroma and their flavour and their perfume, all inextricably mixed and mingled with the almost pure alcohol that had arisen over the months and the years to lie

138

fermenting on the top of the bottle and hence in the bottom of his glass . . .

He made a great effort, to his eternal credit, and tried again.

'In view of what you have just told me about your village,' he pronounced carefully, 'may I ask you for a little information. You have two characters here, Seylan the garage-man and Cardin, a farmer. Both of them bear a remarkable resemblance to the late Edmond Laroche, the famous jeweller in the Rue de La Paix.'

The man looked at him without any noticeable change of expression.

'Yes. Everyone here knows that.'

'And it is accepted?'

'Of course. Why not? Why should it not be accepted? They have two different names for the simple reason that Madame Laroche, with her money and connections, is able to control two-thirds of the Chamber of Deputies – although everyone in the village knows who their father was. They are well established, thanks to her, and have all the power, the wealth and the influence of the old lady behind them.

'But they are bad characters, both of them – just like their father. Bad blood will always out. If I were you, m'sieu, I would not have anything to do with either of them.'

Now that, M. Pinaud thought swiftly, was a fair and comprehensive statement of fact. He had asked for information, knowing full well what the answer would be before he heard it. But that was one of the most fascinating aspects of his profession – a mass of familiar and therefore useless knowledge with sometimes, concealed amongst it, the one small fact of

139

vital importance . . .

This time he had not been lucky. Everything that the proprietor had told him he already knew. But there might have been something else, some information of urgent importance. He had to try. For this he was paid. An honest man at least always tried to earn his salary.

The proprietor looked at him thoughtfully before he continued to speak.

'Look, m'sieu,' he said, quietly and earnestly, 'you seem like a good and sympathetic type to me. You appreciate the good food this establishment sells you, and you obviously enjoy your wine and liqueur.

'My advice to you, therefore, is to cut your losses — whatever they may have been down here — and get back to the big city, from which you came, as fast as you can.

'I can tell you — and not only tell you but prove it to you if you wish — that others have tried to tangle with these two in the past. Always with the same result. All have come off second-best.

'Here in this village you have money, influence and loyalty — and ties of blood. Such a combination is unbeatable. I could tell you tales that would make your hair curl. But perhaps I had better not. I would like to welcome you again as a client.'

M. Pinaud took a hearty swallow of that astonishing liqueur and reassured him with the sincerity his generosity deserved.

'Thank you for your good advice, m'sieu,' he said. 'From what I have seen and experienced, I know it to be excellent. May I take this opportunity of thanking you, not only for your wise counsel, but also for your courtesy and your generosity.

'Now, if you will just allow me to pay, in addition to my bill, for two more glasses of this superb liqueur, I will take your advice, leave this village and go home.'

'But this bottle is the hospitality of the house —'

'Nonsense — you have already proved your point. Now accept one last drink from a grateful and satisfied client. You never know — I might have to come back again some time to Valoisin.'

The proprietor smiled cheerfully and filled their glasses again.

'Well,' he said, 'since you put it so nicely — I hope you will.'

M. Pinaud took another hearty swallow of that remarkable liqueur and stood up.

'Then,' he said, 'if you would be kind enough to let me have my bill and show me the way to the kitchen so that I can thank and congratulate Madame your wife on her superb cooking, I will be on my way.'

'Certainly, m'sieu. She will be overjoyed. Not many clients have such a charming and considerate thought.'

Having delighted Madame with his enthusiastic thanks and appreciation of such a memorable meal, he finished his drink as he waited for his bill and then left the inn.

He remembered, with vivid clarity, what he had thought recently while he was in the garage.

The fewer people in this village — with all its blood-ties and loyalties sustained and pumped, lubricated and guided by the flow of unlimited money — the fewer people who knew what he was doing the better. This he had proved, the hard way.

He would go back home by train, one unidentified unit in the midst of hundreds of others, one individual unobserved and so unrecognised, one person – even if noted, recorded and described on the telephone – who could travel safely in a vast company, anonymous and unknown.

'Excuse me, m'sieu,' he asked politely, 'but could you tell me where I can get a 'bus to the railway station? I understand that it is quite a way out.'

The old man eyed him with compassion. He had clear and merry blue eyes, a thick mane of snow-white hair and a face like a brown and wrinkled walnut. His smile, despite false teeth which looked as though they had been made in error for an entirely different person, was a singularly charming one.

'Why, of course,' he replied. 'It comes along this very High Street and the driver has instructions to stop for whoever hails it.'

'Thank you very much.'

'But that is on a Tuesday,' the old man continued cheerfully, watching his crestfallen features with an impish glee. 'And to-day is not Tuesday.'

'You mean to say –'

'Yes. Once a week. Only on Tuesdays. If you insist on going up by train to the big city, then Tuesday is when you go. Mind you, our rates are not as high as in many other places. And who in their right senses, anyway, would want to go to a place like Paris after living in the country? A lunatic, perhaps. But certainly not any sane and normal person.

'Here in the country we have birds nesting in hedges, fields with cattle and trees in the forests. We have bird-song at dawn and dusk, and peace and silence at night.

'In the city you have stinks and noise and people

142

crawling like ants. You walk on stone between shops — not on grass and good earth — and you have to look before you dare step into the road.'

His argument was so logical and so persuasive that M. Pinaud felt an overwhelming sense of guilt and thought that he was really under an obligation to justify his extraordinary desire.

'I have very important business there,' he said, pleading with great sincerity to justify his mental equilibrium. 'I also happen to live there with my wife and family. I had an accident in my car, in which I drove here early this morning, and the repairs will take some time. I would naturally like to spend the night at home with my wife and children.'

The old man regarded him with undisguised approval. This, for one of another generation, appeared to have his head screwed on in the right way. His reasons were both cogent and logical. To encounter such a type these days was a rarity. Even an exception.

The brown and wrinkled features creased into the beginnings of that charming smile and, since he did not open his lips to disclose the false teeth which had been made so skilfully and so successfully by some incompetent dentist to fit another person with an entirely different physiognomy, the general effect was one of courteous approval, which heartened and encouraged M. Pinaud, after his shattering and un-expected disappointment, to a considerable degree.

Why not walk?' the old man asked him, with a warm and comforting friendliness in his voice. 'The station is not far — just outside the village. I walk every day of my life. That is why I keep so healthy and so fit. Walking is the finest exercise the human body can have. It was designed and evolved by nature

143

to walk. That is why walking must be beneficial.

'Mind you, I have to spend about one tenth of my pension – which is not a large one – on rubber heels for all my shoes, since the synthetic plastic rubbish they sell as rubber these days lasts two or three weeks at the most – but then, since I enjoy good health at my age, only an idiot would grumble.

'Take my advice, young man – you do the same. Buy rubber heels and start walking. You will find it well worth while.'

As advice, M. Pinaud thought swiftly, it was wise, sound and practical. For all the good he was doing towards the solving of this Laroche case he might just as well be walking.

This decision would be bound to please the economical mind of M. le Chef. Especially if he ever found out that after a lunch which had lasted for the duration of nearly three hours, there was an item of a taxi-fare on his employee's expense-sheet from the village of Valoisin to the station, for the purpose of catching a train in order to get back to Paris in a hurry . . .

He shuddered at the nightmare scenes his vivid imagination immediately evolved and pictured, terrifying in their reality and intensity, and made a swift and conclusive decision to adopt this courteous old gentleman's suggestion, take his advice and walk immediately to the station.

After all – what was the cost of a pair of new rubber heels? How often had he spent far more than that on a bottle of not particualrly outstanding wine?

The clerk in the booking-office was seated comfortably at a long table, well away from the window, very busily occupied in filling in forms.

So intent, so busy, so comfortable and so pre-occupied was he in this labour, that he did not even trouble to look up until M. Pinaud, losing patience at being ignored whilst standing there, rapped sharply and loudly on the glass of the window.

After all, he thought, there might well be a train due at any moment and he had no intention of missing it just because this individual did not seem to understand the primary functions of his employment.

So he continued with his rapping, energetically and forcibly, until the man, slowly and with extreme reluctance, finally forced himself out of his comfortable chair and came towards the window.

And then all he said was: 'Yes?'

Now on M. Pinaud, who had been very strictly brought up at home by old-fashioned parents, to whom courtesy was one of the cardinal virtues of living, this attitude and indifference had, naturally and inevitably, something of the effect of a red rag on a bull.

After all, he was here at this station for one simple and easily predictable purpose – namely, to buy a ticket with the object of travelling on the railway. An uncomplicated business transaction. Which, incidentally, paid the salary of this moron who sold the ticket. Some show of good manners, some little courtesy – even a polite good-afternoon – would not have called for much effort, he reflected – and how much more pleasant would that have been.

'A third single to Paris,' he said curtly. 'How much and when is the next train due?'

The clerk looked up at the wall-clock and then at him. The old man in the High Street had looked at him with compassion. Here through the chipped and battered glass of the window he could easily distinguish several emotions, but compassion was definitely not one of them.

On these thin and spiteful features there was hostility, at being disturbed from his peaceful and relaxing occupation of form-filling during the quiet hours of the afternoon. There was satisfaction at the undoubted dismay his forthcoming information would inevitably bring. And there was also triumph in the forthcoming fact that this arrogant Parisian bastard would shortly be cut down to size, whoever he was.

'You have just missed the one you should have taken, m'sieu,' he announced cheerfully and triumphantly. And yet – perhaps because of something even his self-centred absorption could not fail to read in the hard eyes confronting him – he made an effort and took great care to retain civility in his voice in addition to these other two inflections.

'You have now some two hours and forty minutes to wait for the next.'

'What?'

'Yes. And this is only a two-coach pay-train, stopping at every halt and station as far as Lapalisse, where you will have to change to pick up the main-line, P.L.M. to Paris.'

And then, perhaps because converstion with another human being came as a welcome diversion from the long and lonely hours of form-filling, his monosyllabic and discourteous gambit, which had expanded unaided into sentences of normal speech, now suddenly – as if bursting the flood-gates of some devious psychological inhibition – became a torrent of eloquence.

146

With his face jammed up against the plate-glass, the words seemed to pour through the spaced louvres in an unending and unstoppable flow.

'Yes – and what is more it is perfectly obvious why. You see, this station has been scheduled for closure for the past ten years, so you can be perfectly certain that one day some *fonctionnaire* sitting on his fat arse in a plush office with three secretaries will sign the right form and then it finally will be closed. That is only normal. That is the first law of economics. What does not pay must cease to function – whether you are talking about a stall in the Flea Market, a tart on the Boul' Mich' or a broker's office on the *Bourse*.

'This branch-line to Valoisin no longer pays, therefore it will be closed. People now have cars and do not need trains. Before they earned enough money to buy cars and needed the trains there were still never any trains at this time in the afternoon. People who wanted to go to Paris went in the morning and came back in the evening. Which gave them a whole day in the city. Then there was a good service. Especially on Tuesdays with the 'bus. Who in their right senses would possibly want to go to the city at this time in the afternoon?'

This was clearly a rhetorical question, neither needing nor demanding an answer, since the overwhelming spate of words never faltered nor ceased, but the expression in his eyes made it perfectly clear that the answer – even if unspoken – was obviously only lunatics like you.

At this juncture, M. Pinaud's chronicler (who is only concerned with the truth) feels it incumbent upon him to point out to the more discerning of his readers, not only the admirable restraint but also the

147

exceptional duration of his hero's patience, in the hope that he will not be the only one to appreciate it in the interval of waiting for posterity eventually and unanimously to recognise it.

All M. Pinaud wanted to do was to get back home as quickly as possible in order to participate in the riotous joys of the evening bath of his two young daughters.

Fond relatives had bought them giant ducks, frogs, paddle-wheels and massive sponges – all with the capability of creating immense splashes on a floor the donors would never be obliged to wipe up – and it was always a debatable question, his wife was wont to declare, as to who enjoyed the bath more . . .

What on earth was he doing here, he asked himself – wasting his time with this idiot, who looked as if he were firmly determined to go on talking and enjoying doing so for the next two hours and forty minutes, until the train eventually came in.

All he wanted to do was to get home. Here he was wasting valuable time. Quickly he stuffed the money he had taken out for his ticket back into his pocketbook, thanked the clerk politely – which he felt was more than he deserved – and left the booking-hall.

He would hitch-hike home.

Other people, including young relatives possessed of an unbounded faith, trust and confidence – not only in themselves but in the world at large – had assured him repeatedly that this was the only logical and modern method of transport from A to B. No fuss. No responsibility. No expense. And they had told him the correct sign to give with the thumb.

So he would try it himself. Why not?

ELEVEN

Germaine looked at him with concern.

'I am very tired,' he said simply.

He was late, exhausted and obviously mentally distressed. His face was scratched.

In his eyes there was that dull look of apathy she hated to see — a look compounded in some indefinable and yet unmistakable way of pain, bitterness and a resigned acceptance. A look to her all the more moving in that it was so tragically uncharacteristic of him.

She remembered how seldom she had seen it before during that astonishing sequence of apparently insoluble and yet triumphantly solved cases which had coincided with all the years of their married life.

And so she changed her mind and when she spoke her words were entirely different from what she had been about to say. First things should come first.

She smiled at him, and the love in her eyes seemed to warm his heart with a comforting glow.

'You are late,' she said cheerfully. 'But not too late. The children agreed to wait for their bath, and we have had a wonderful time for the past hour betting *centimes* as to where the hand of the clock would be when you arrived.'

So the rubber ducks were hurled in and out of the bath and from the frogs and the sponges the water splashed and dripped all over the floor, the taps were turned on and off, the drain-plug pulled out to see who would be the quickest to put it back, and a good time was had by all.

For the first time that day he felt relaxed and happy. He could feel the hard knot of tension and strain almost physically melting in the radiance of the love and tenderness that encompassed his family.

When eventually the children were tucked into bed, warm, cuddly and sleepy, he burst into the kitchen and swept his wife off her feet into his arms.

'What a wonderful smell — what is it? I am hungry. I am famished. I am starving.'

The omelette, the chicken and the cheese at Valoisin were obviously now only a memory.

'Then I suggest you put me down so that I can do something about it. I made you one of my special casseroles. It is the only thing I can keep hot when I don't know what time you are coming home. I have just added some more gravy. It will be ready when you have finished your drink.'

'Thank you. What a lovely wife I have.'

He obeyed at once. If he really extracted his digit and moved swiftly he could make it considerably more than the one drink she fondly imagined he would have. After his experiences of hitch-hiking he felt definitely in need of a few very quick ones.

He was doing something about this when Germaine called out from the kitchen.

'There was a telephone message for you about an hour ago. Louise de Granson from Laroche. She was his secretary, you told me.'

He paused and tensed with the glass halfway to his lips.

'Yes. What did she want?'

'She said she saw you at Valoisin to-day and would like you to call at the shop in the Rue de La Paix this evening when you come home. She will be working late.'

'Did she say what time?'

'No. It does not matter when — as long as you go there this evening. It is important. She said to ring the bell at the side if the shop is closed. You know where it is as apparently you have been there before.'

'Yes, I have.'

He emptied his glass in one gigantic swallow. This was only cheap grocer's sherry — all he could afford on the microscopic salary M. le Chef paid him — but if one consumed enough there was an undeniable effect.

'Well then,' he called out cheerfully to the kitchen, 'that is good news. There is no need for me to rush about like a mad dog for nothing. I shall have plenty of time to eat that delicious casserole you have been making for me. I can smell it in here. When I have finished it I will go there and see what she wants.'

'Right. It won't be long now. I'll give you a call.'

'Thank you. If it tastes like it smells I shall eat it all.'

'Good. You must be hungry. It is getting late.'

Which meant, he reflected sadly as he refilled his glass swiftly and efficiently, that there was very little valuable drinking time left.

Admittedly, this was only a cheap and second-class drink, but perhaps if he drank enough of it some — in its passage through his liquor-impregnated duodenum and ileum — might well meet and mingle with the

151

remaining drops of that remarkable liqueur and exquisite wine he had imbibed for lunch, and thereby, during the course of the miracle of digestion, might even perchance partake of something of their quality, improving its own in the process . . .

This was a truly exhilarating thought, considering what he had paid the grocer for a litre bottle.

Like all practical demonstrations of any scientific theory, each experiment is bound to use the materials and ingredients involved. To prove that water is a poor conductor of heat, a piece of ice is placed in one end of a long glass test-tube and remains unmelted while the water in the other end, aided by the flame of a Bunsen burner, boils away happily and strongly.

M. Pinaud was on his second bottle of sherry when the call came from the kitchen.

He admitted to himself, with characteristic honesty, that his experiment had failed, his theory had not been proved, his exhilarating thought had perhaps been a fond illusion, and that his grocer had definitely been overpaid.

The taxi pulled up in the Rue de La Paix outside the closed and shuttered premises of Laroche the jewellers.

M. Pinaud paid the driver, thanked him politely, congratulated him on his skill, added a carefully calculated regulation tip and watched him drive off without regret.

Then he entered the amount in his notebook under that week's expenses. M. le Chef would no doubt fly into a vile passion, but that was not his fault. The salary with which his strenuous efforts were rewarded inevitably resulted in the location of his flat being some considerable distance from the Rue de La Paix, where behind those locked and impenetrable steel shutters lay a stock worth millions of francs.

After all, he reflected philosophically as he rang the bell on the side door, it was still his case. No-one had removed him from it yet. And his car had been wrecked in the course of duty. Therefore a taxi-fare became naturally a legitimate expense.

These comforting reflections were interrupted by the opening of the door.

Louise de Granson gave him a charming smile and pulled her quilted housecoat tighter.

'M'sieu Pinaud — how good of you to come. Inside quickly — it has turned cold. Please close the door.'

She turned and climbed the narrow steep stairs. The doors of her office and the adjoining one were both shut. Without hesitation she walked along the passage and led the way up another short flight of stairs, through an open door into the lounge of a luxuriously furnished flat.

The far door was wide-open. Through the aperture there came the rich aroma of percolating coffee from the kitchen.

She walked straight on, waving one hand as she went.

'Try the settee,' she said. 'You will find it very comfortable. Coffee is ready.'

'Thank you. You are very kind.'

He stood watching the back of the quilted house-coat in amazement until he was alone.

This was an altogether different person from the Louise de Granson he remembered. Gone was the efficient and qualified secretary to the jeweller with an international reputation — here was a beautiful woman, intimately seductive, obviously passionate and radiating charm and an overwhelming sexual appeal.

This was something he could not understand.

Then he sat down in front of the glowing electric fire with a sigh of relief. She had been right, it was a supremely comfortable settee. The arms were wide, and on each was an ash-tray.

He pulled out his packet of cigarettes.

'Do you mind if I smoke?' he called out.

'Of course not. Would you like a cigar?'

'No, thank you. I prefer a cigarette.'

'Are they strong?'

'Yes. Gauloises.'

'Then I will have one of yours when I come in. Just a few minutes longer.'

'There is no hurry,' he replied politely as he lit a cigarette.

He smoked with tranquil relaxation, watching all the time the open doorway to the kitchen.

When she appeared in the opening, carrying a large tray in both hands, he saw that she was no longer wearing the housecoat. He also noticed that through the open chiffon *négligée* edged with Brussels lace which partly covered the transparent nightgown beneath, he could clearly see, above and below the tray – thanks to the powerful bulb illuminating the kitchen – every line and contour of her exquisite body as she walked towards him into the lounge.

On the tray there were cups and saucers, a coffee-pot, milk, sugar and cream, two large wine-glasses and a bottle of noble *cognac*.

But all this, his chronicler (who is concerned only with the truth) is bound in all fairness to admit, his

154

eyes saw only when she stopped walking towards him with the light behind her and sat down in the other corner of the settee, having placed the tray carefully on a small table already in position between them.

She gave him another charming smile and held out one hand.

'May I have one of your strong cigarettes, M'sieu Pinaud?'

'Of course.'

He offered his packet, lit one for her and took another for himself.

'Thank you. How do you like your coffee — milk or cream?'

He gestured with his cigarette.

'With that label in front of me,' he replied without hesitation, 'the answer is black.'

She laughed. It was a lovely laugh, he thought — deep, rich and happy. A laugh truly worthy of her. A laugh he had never heard before. He had seen her smile, he remembered, when he had first met her and spoken to her, but he had never heard her laugh before.

Then she poured the coffee and filled the two glasses almost to the brim.

'If you pull that table a little nearer,' she said, 'you will be able to reach more easily.'

'Thank you,' he replied politely and did so. Then he tasted and sipped a little of the *cognac*. It was exquisite — aged and matured to perfection. It flowed in a velvet incandescence down his throat and he seemed to feel its glowing warmth like outspreading and comforting fingers reaching tenderly, soothingly and comfortingly to caress every part of his inside. And as if that were not enough, the enticing richness even seemed to surge up into his mind . . .

155

But then he was a man with imagination.

'I saw you when I left the *Château* to-day, M'sieu Pinaud,' she said.

With a great effort he forced himself to listen. It was not easy.

'You came when I was in conference with Madame Laroche. She and her money have a controlling interest in the firm. Her object now – I should in all fairness use two different words – her main aim and ambition – is to keep the shop open and profitable. In spite of what has happened.'

He drank a little coffee, which was delightfully strong and scalding hot. He lifted his glass and saw that it was empty.

'Please help yourself,' she said, and then continued without a pause. 'You can imagine how these police enquiries you have been making could be damaging to the hitherto unblemished reputation of the firm, which has traded here in these premises under the same name since 1715. Any scandal about the death of Edmond would be fatal – unthinkable.'

He had refilled his glass at her invitation. Now he drank a little more of that superb brandy, his mind so filed with concentrated thought that he did not even taste it.

He set the glass down on the tray and turned to look at her.

'Then that is why I have accidents whenever I go to Valoisin,' he said slowly.

The cool grey eyes met his frankly.

'Of course. But I told them that methods such as those were far too crude for a man like you.'

'You were quite right.'

'I knew I was right. I am usually right. That is why

156

you are sitting here to-night beside me on this settee.

'I am asking you now to finish with this investigation, which can do no good and perhaps untold harm to many people. Whatever your price, we are willing to pay it. There is unlimited money available – you know that. Say the word and you can be rich beyond your dreams.

'And – as you have already guessed – there are other things as well. They go with the money.'

There was no need for her to go into more detail. It was unnecessary for her to elaborate with more words. Her meaning, as she moved her body lasciviously under its transparent covering, had already been clear and obvious in each and every one of her provocative glances as well as in the cadence and the innuendo in her voice. This was woman incarnate – the eternal seducer – the essence of temptation . . .

Desire tore at him with the pain of sharp claws – so keen, so vital, so excruciating, it almost became physical – desire and plain unadulterated lust tormented him with the ecstasy of pain – desire seemed to consume him with a longing and a yearning that was like the burning of a flame.

He swiftly emptied his glass and almost in the same movement refilled it and drank again.

Amidst the turmoil and the confusion of that raging sea which was the welter of his thoughts, one conviction seemed to thrust up like an impregnable and indestructible rock – that it was a sin and a shame to waste such noble *cognac*. He was honest enough to admit to himself that in spite of swallowing it he could not even taste it.

The settee might have been – and probably still was – comfortable, but it was an undeniable and indisputable fact that he was not.

Instinctively he moved. Her eyes met his, understanding, approving and confident . . .

Abruptly he stood up, and immediately her already reaching hand withdrew.

'Look,' he said quietly, 'if I feel like it, I can go out of here, walk fifty metres, and buy whatever type of body I prefer. Admittedly not so beautiful, not so lovely, not so desirable, as yours. But with a difference. With one important difference.

'To none of them are any strings or conditions attached.'

She did not answer.

Every time he looked at her he felt his desire surging, his control weakening. Then stop looking at her, you idiot, he told himself savagely. Think of your wife. Think of your children. You have got to fight. You have got to win. If you accept — how can you possibly live with yourself and your conscience afterwards?

Have you done the right thing, he thought. If you were prepared, he addressed himself sternly, to tell M. le Chef to stuff his job — which was and had been your whole life — up his backside, which you did in his office, while you continued, in spite of official orders to the contrary, to try to find this murderer, then surely you must have enough moral courage to refuse this chance and haphazard fornication — so freely and so delightfully offered — in order to honour your principles and retain your self-respect as a man.

He stood there beside the settee, ignoring her once again outstretched hand, a figure — completely unconscious of it — somehow proudly majestic with the innate dignity of his convictions.

158

Then he spoke again.

'Mademoiselle de Granson, I have work to do. And I am going to do it. Someone murdered Edmond Laroche and I am going to find out who it was.'

Still she did not answer.

Now here his chronicler (who is only concerned with the truth) feels compelled in all fairness to point out – if only to silence those carping critics who sometimes seek to denigrate his hero – the fantastic extent and positively awesome implications of M. Pinaud's abnegation.

For all this, he would like to stress, happened in the days when M. Pinaud was a younger man of exceptional virility, normally aroused, excited and inflamed by the sight of the unclothed female form – and a long time before the remorseless and relentless years of time had brought him to that inevitable stage and state when a good book and a pipe appeared so much more peaceful, definitely preferable and certainly less exhausting . . .

'I will say good-night now,' he continued in that same quiet voice whose tones were to seemingly chime and reverberate in her head long after he had gone.

'I am sorry that you should have had to waste your time. I can find my own way out – there is no need for you to come down again. Thank you for the coffee – it was quite the best I have ever tasted.'

Then he opened the door, went out and left her alone.

He would go home, he thought as he walked down the deserted street. He would go home to Germaine his wife.

159

He would create a son — even two sons. Now — and only now — he was just beginning to taste that magnificent *cognac*. Now he felt in the mood. Or perhaps it was — and always had been — the same mood. Transference of object, not of subject.

His thoughts were a welter of confusion, his mind a turmoil of conflicting and confusing emotion.

A man should have a son, or even better — two sons. So that whatever little of condemnation in his character — which he had inherited from his own father — would not die. Girls were all very well — and a lovable comfort in old age — but a man needed a son so that when he died perhaps something of himself — perhaps the better part — might have a chance to live on . . .

He kept on walking and walking and walking.

He was tired out and exhausted by what had been a very long and arduous day. If he put in an expense-claim for a taxi-fare to see Louise de Granson on official business concerned with the murder of her late employer, Edmond Laroche, it was surely reasonable to expect that M. le Chef was bound to accept another claim for the return fare, in order to get him home well after the regulation working hours even of the *Sûreté*.

The trouble was that there were no taxis about. The streets were deserted.

What would he tell his wife? There had never been any secrets between them before, in all the years of an ideally happy marriage. Now to save her distress and unhappiness he would have to keep one.

Should he tell her anything? Life was a matter of compromise. That was why he found it so difficult to conform. He was by nature an idealist, a perfec-

160

tionist. To him everything had to be as right as he could imagine it. Which in this life was impossible. There was always an eternal and remorseless balance — good and evil, day with light and night with darkness, sorrow and sadness, happiness and grief. Joy and laughter follow the tears, thankfulness eradicates the bitterness, happiness unfolds like a flower to soothe the agony of the sharp thorns of pain . . .

He continued to walk.

He thought about this remarkable case in which he had done so little. He remembered the interviews he had had with the Capet family. In his vivid imagination he saw them again — father, mother, son and daughter. All of them concerned and implicated with a swine who had once been Edmond Laroche, and who was now a corpse.

He walked on and on. It was a long way. He could not afford to live anywhere near the Rue de La Paix. He was tired, but he walked on. He wanted to get back to the peace, the love and the security that transformed a cheap flat into an ideal and happy home. And therefore beside such things his fatigue and his exhaustion were as nothing.

There was something about that interview with Yvonne, the daughter of Capet. There was something he felt that he ought to remember. There had been something important at the time — but now it eluded him. He was too tired to think.

He burst into the hall with a sigh of relief. It was good to be home.

There was no need to tell her everything. There was no need to distress her needlessly by recounting all the details of his perfectly normal and completely understandable lust.

161

He would play it down. He would compromise, as throughout his life he had been compelled to do. And in the morning, in spite of his exhaustion, he would get up early and go to see Yvonne Capet before he reported to M. le Chef.

'Would you like some coffee?' Germaine called out from the kitchen. 'It will not take a minute.'

'Thank you very much. That is just what I need. She gave me some, but it was not as nice as yours.'

He lied unblushingly, just to make her happy. Small and clever lies were more than the very foundations of a happy marriage. They were the keystones and the arches of the complete edifice.

'What did she want?'

He came into the kitchen, tall and masterful, his weariness forgotten. And he told her the truth.

'She wanted me to go to bed with her, as a reward for not doing my duty.'

She could not tell if he were joking. His features were inscrutable, his voice expressionless.

'And did you?'

'Of course not. Why should I?'

'You said she was beautiful.'

He reached out quickly and took her hands.

There were tiny lines at the corners of her eyes — a legacy from that nightmare time when their youngest child had caught whooping-cough when a few weeks old and she had stayed up with her night after night while he had been away on a case, to pick her up each time she coughed. And so to save her life.

And the hands he held in his own were rough with years of washing and scrubbing and cleaning and cooking for two small children.

'Nothing like as beautiful or as lovely as you,' he

162

said quietly and in a tone she had seldom heard before.

And at the love and the tenderness in his voice she caught her breath with emotion and turned away to the coffee-pot lest he see the tears in her eyes.

He released her hands.

'Why should I?' he repeated gently. 'I can go and I am now going to bed with you. You are my wife. I have conjugal rights. That is the law. So hurry up with that coffee-pot and do not dare to deny them, or else I shall take you to court.'

TWELVE

Early next morning Capet was surprised to see him.

'M'sieu Pinaud – but I am just going off to work –'

His voice stopped abruptly. Nevertheless he opened wide the front door of the flat and stepped back.

'Come inside.'

'Thank you. I will not keep you a moment,' M. Pinaud told him. 'Just one question for you, and then I would like to see your daughter Yvonne. How did you get on with Madame Laroche?'

'Very well. She has promised to help with the child.'

'Good.'

'Yes. That is a great anxiety taken from my mind. I found her very gracious and most helpful.'

M. Pinaud felt like telling him that his own experiences with her had been somewhat different, but decided not to prolong the conversation. The man was obviously eager to leave, and restrained only by his innate courtesy and good manners.

'I am glad to hear it,' he said quietly. 'Now if I could have a few words with your daughter, I will not detain you any longer.'

'Of course. Come in here and sit down. I will tell her. Then – if you would excuse me – I must run. I shall be at home here to-night if you would like to see me.'

He left the room and closed the door.

When it opened and Yvonne came in, M. Pinaud, who had sat down, immediately stood up and offered her the chair, which was the only comfortable one in the room.

'Please sit down, Mademoiselle Capet. I am sorry to disturb you so early, but I will not keep you long.'

His voice was kind and courteous. He pulled up a small chair and sat down opposite her.

'You are not disturbing me, M'sieu Pinaud. I have been up for hours. What is it you want? I thought I had told you everything the last time we met.'

'You did. I am sorry to reopen the wound, but there is something I must know.'

'What is that?'

'You told me that Edmond Laroche loved you and intended to marry you.'

'Yes.'

Just the one word, low and heavy, but filled with countless echoes of pain and grief and sorrow.

'How can you be so certain? Did he ever actually tell you? Did you discuss the subject together? Have you any proof?'

She closed her eyes for a moment, as if in thought. Then she opened them and shook her head.

'No. But it was understood.'

'What exactly do you mean by that?'

She waited for a long moment and then spoke without hesitation.

'We were in a night-club once. Some man at the next table made an offensive remark about me. I always remember what Edmond said after he hit him

165

in the mouth. "This is the young lady who has honoured me by consenting to become my wife. Your insults are therefore unpardonable. I sincerely hope that I have broken your jaw. At least it may stop you from making filthy remarks for some time to come." '

The slow, quiet and tragic voice ceased. But in her eyes as she spoke of Edmond Laroche he could see the love, the trust and the happiness shining and glowing as if with a life of their own.

They sat there for some moments together, and to the girl his silence was the most sympathetic thing she had known for days.

After a long while she broke it. He had waited deliberately, wishing her to be the first one to speak.

'That is what I meant when I said that it was understood. That was the first — but not the last occasion on which he used the word wife. I thanked him and never referred to the matter again.

'I do not pretend to understand how or why such a situation could gradually evolve between two people, become acceptable and remain recognised — all without discussion. But it did. You must believe me. I can assure you that it did.'

Her voice died as her mind fled back to her memories.

Again he did not speak. He continued to sit there, with understanding and compassion in his eyes, his silence an acceptance, a sympathy and a tolerance.

When she spoke again her voice was soft and hesitant with conjecture.

'This is something I can never explain. I try — but there is no-one to tell me if I am right. And now it does not matter any more.

'It might have been because I was a virgin. I had

never known a man before. This fact might well have made a profound impression on a man like Edmond – oh, I came to know and understand him well. I am not an idiot, in spite of being brought up so strictly here at home. I knew him for what he was – and accepted him. And forgave him and loved him.'

'You must have loved him very greatly.'

Even as M. Pinaud spoke, he wondered what had made him say that. Perhaps as an encouragement, since her sorrow – to one of his inordinate sensitivity – was a torment to watch. But he had no regrets. His intuition had been right. He was thankful that he had succeeded.

Her eyes brightened with a momentary animation.

'There is only one way to love, M'sieu Pinaud – completely, wholly and unreservedly. To him, I was like someone from another world. All his life he had been used to the other type – to those who ran after him not for what he was, but for all the things his money could buy. Perhaps it was the contrast that made him think – that changed his mind. I do not know. And now I shall never know. It does not matter any more.'

And then the slow tears came to blind her eyes – agonising in their memories and yet healing in their release of so much pent-up emotion – and she raised her hands to cover her face.

He stood up in one swift and powerful movement and laid one strong hand with infinite gentleness on her brow.

'Courage, Yvonne,' he whispered, in a voice that was unsteady with the intensity of his own feelings. 'You will have more than any of the others. You will have a son to remember him by.'

Then he left her to her tears and let himself out of the flat alone, without seeing anyone else.

From Capet's flat he took an omnibus to the Rue de La Paix, entering the fare methodicially in his notebook.

M. le Chef would not be pleased, but there was nothing he could do about it. He might even rejoice that owing to the integrity of his employee it was not a taxi-fare, as it had been the night before.

But now there was no hurry. The omnibus would get him there soon enough.

At the side entrance of the shop he rang the bell. He was not in the mood to listen to any more of the pontifical utterances of M. Dubois the manager.

Clad in a plain black skirt and a white frilled blouse — and therefore seeming an entirely different person — Louise de Granson looked at him with calm astonishment.

'Well — M'sieu Pinaud — you are the last person I ever expected.'

'I can quite understand that,' he replied quietly. 'Could you spare me a few moments?'

'Of course. Come on up.'

The office was unchanged. But the roses in the bowl were fresh and glorious and their arrangement as beautiful and as tasteful as before.

She sat down at the desk and waved him to the nearest chair by the table.

'Well now, M'sieu Pinaud — what can I do for you?'

Her voice was completely expressionless.

This was in the morning. This was a private office in the premises of Laroche the jewellers. The flat above, the settee, the *cognac* and the *négligée* of the

168

night before might never have existed.

He hesitated. This was not going to be easy. After – or perhaps because of last night – he himself, usually so self-assured and confident, now felt suddenly lost and confused.

'Tell me,' he said, and even as he began to speak, slowly and hesitatingly, he felt a sudden surge of confidence and knew that he was right. 'Tell me, Mademoiselle de Granson, a little more about yourself, about your background and about your life here with the late Edmond Laroche.'

She looked at him enigmatically, but there was no hesitation in her reply. The beginning of a smile softened the corners of her wide and sensitive mouth, but this she immediately controlled.

'I am afraid there is not very much to tell, M'sieu Pinaud,' she said. 'I was fortunate in having a very expensive and very exclusive education, as befitted the daughter of an Admiral.

After that I came to Paris to find some employment that would appeal to me. I have always been very interested in jewellery. A mutual friend introduced me to Edmond Laroche, who said he needed a secretary. My references and my school record were satisfactory. Madame Laroche approved of my manners. And so I came here.

'After a few weeks I began to go to night-classes.'

'For what?'

'To take a course in gemmology.'

'Why did you do that?'

'I thought I might be of more use to him, especially in doing such complicated things as valuations for probate or insurance.'

He looked at her thoughtfully.

'Were you in love with him?' he asked quietly.

The cool grey eyes met his frankly, without confusion, without fear, without prevarication.

'Of course I was. That is why I did it. Edmond — like so many bad characters — was a genius. He needed help.

'He went to Switzerland himself to find and organise that primitive family who made those singing birdboxes. Until he went there they had never sold one ouside their own country. He designed and sketched the boxes himself and then had them mounted and set with precious stones here in Paris by one of the master manufacturing jewellers in the trade.'

'You admit that he was a bad character, then?'

'Of course I do. Of course he was. I was quite prepared to condone his behaviour. I suppose such an attitude of mind depends on the way one is brought up — by which standards behaviour is assessed, measured and judged. Here was a qualified and expert gemmologist, master of his craft, well worthy of his world-wide reputation — surely he was entitled to sow his wild oats.'

She paused for a moment and sighed before she continued.

'I would have been quite happy — as soon as I came here — to be his mistress. They said he was a sex maniac. I think I could have coped with that.

'What part does sex play in the happiness of a marriage? A very small one. There are so many other, seemingly insignificant things, which added together — because they happen every moment and every hour — are of infinitely greater importance.

'Most women who marry have to take a chance — have to gamble on that part of their husbands they

170

do not know. That is what makes it the most exciting adventure of all.'

Again he looked at her thoughtfully before he spoke.

'I have met and spoken to Yvonne Capet, Mademoiselle de Granson. Did it ever occur to you that he might have fallen genuinely in love with her?'

Without waiting for her answer he continued to speak.

'This apparently often happens to middle-aged *roués* who are satiated by their excesses – the young, fresh and unsophisticated response of a virgin provides a contrast unexpected enough to act as a powerful stimulant. It is not difficult to imagine how an innocent and vital eagerness to experience all the thrills and romance of an entirely different life could stir the pride of a man who held the keys to that life so easily in his hands.'

He paused and waited. She looked at him calmly before she spoke.

'It is not surprising that you should suggest that. I know that Capet had been putting pressure on him recently to marry his daughter. But I also know that Edmond got one of his pleasures from hurting people. That was his nature.

'You are quite right, M'sieu Pinaud – how you know I have no idea. But Edmond was, as you say, genuinely and sincerely in love with Yvonne Capet and intended to marry her. This he told me. And yet he derived a perverse pleasure and a sadistic satisfaction by insulting her father and not telling him. He was that kind of man.

'Always he did what he liked. He would reject suggestions, advice, help – anything – so that he could

171

enjoy the exhilarating satisfaction of having his own way.'

There was a long silence.

'And yet you loved him?'

His voice was gentle, sad and quiet. Her reply followed with so little hesitation that it could have been part of the same sentence.

'There is only one way to love, M'sieu Pinaud.'

This was the second time that he had been told the same thing that morning. Strangely and inexplicably, this time the same words seemed somehow to have a far greater meaning, a more profound significance and an even more poignant implication even than those he had heard before.

After a short pause she continued.

'One is thankful for the good and one accepts the evil. Out of both the character is formed. There is no perfection in human nature.'

His voice as he replied was still gentle and quiet. But now in it there was understanding. And sympathy and tolerance as well.

'As you say, there is no perfection. One must accept. But this, Mademoiselle de Granson, you could not do. I heard this morning that he was prepared and willing to marry her. And intended to do so. That is why I came here. I did not understand how you could have known. Now you say that he told you himself.'

He paused for a moment but she did not speak. She just sat there at the desk, perfectly still and motionless, watching him intently.

'And that you could not stand. That you could not condone. That was too hard for you – too hard even for your courage. You of all people – from what you have just told me – would have been prepared to accept, take the risk and marry him. All the years of devoted work you had given him – all for nothing. All your plans and all your hopes – after making yourself indispensable to him in this business – all frustrated because one night a young girl called to deliver an urgent repair and he saw her and desired her.

'And so you killed him – after Capet had left.'

Again he paused. He wished she would say something. The tension was mounting between them, unseen and yet palpable, invisible and yet seemingly tangible.

But still she sat there and did not speak. She reached forward, took up a paper-knife idly and slit open the top envelope on a pile in front of her. But she made no move to take the letter out.

If she refused to speak, he would have to continue. This was his duty. For this he was paid. A man – whatever his employment – should always honour his obligations.

'Anyone could have come up the stairs that evening to the adjoining office – you heard Laroche go down to open the door. Your idea was to shift the blame on to someone else like Capet, convinced that he would have no difficulty in clearing himself. After all – he had no motive. He would not be likely to murder the man he hoped was going to marry his daughter and father her child.

'That would have made it an unsolved crime because there was and could be no proof. That would have left you free to go on here with whoever took over, thus assuring your own future.'

He finished speaking, and it seemed to him, in that moment of almost unbearable tension, that the silence

173

surged up between them and over them, and then came down and buried them, and that they were both alone there, alive and yet buried, and there was nothing but that awful and unending silence above and around them . . .

Quite deliberately she dropped the envelope she had been holding.

Then she placed and held the flat-ended hilt of the paper-knife firmly with both hands against the broad edge of the desk.

Then, suddenly and expectedly, she tensed her muscles and leaned forward in one swift, surging and powerful movement, so that the point and the blade entered her stomach.

He moved as fast as he could, but already he was too late. What he had thought was a paper-knife was in fact a damascened oriental dagger with a short and razor-sharp blade – the weapon that had killed Edmond Laroche.

She was dead by the time he reached her.

Afterwards, with merciless self-condemnation, he always blamed himself for not realising before what she was going to do. That the paper-knife had been completely hidden by pens and pencils in a tray on her desk, and that when he had first gone to her office as directed by M. le Chef he had no cause or reason to suspect her made no difference.

He was at fault. He deserved the blame. He had failed.

He stood there for a long time beside the desk and its dead, listening to the silence and the frightful emptiness beneath it. He felt lost and alone and afraid.

Two rose-petals dropped silently from the bowl on to the table beside the desk.

He closed his eyes and shivered at the pity, the horror and the tragic waste of it all.